The
Missing
Message

The Case of the
MISSING MESSAGE

By Charles Spain Verral

Illustrated by Hamilton Greene

WHITMAN PUBLISHING COMPANY
RACINE, WISCONSIN

To Charlie and Randy
for inspiration

CONTENTS

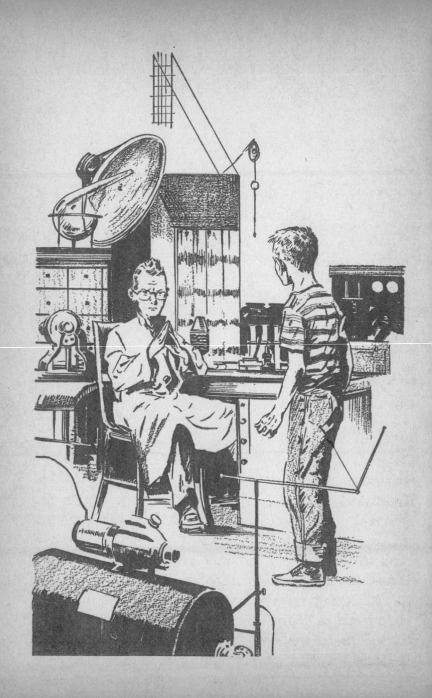

CHAPTER 1

The Mysterious Message

I MIGHT as well explain right away that my name is Jimmy Carson and I live at 43 Maple Street in the town of Crestwood. I'm a detective. And if anybody tries to tell you that a boy like me can't be a real detective and get mixed up in an honest-to-goodness mystery . . . well, I wish he'd been along the night my partner and I investigated the spooky old Madden house.

I still get goose pimples when I think of the terrible shrieks that came from the house, "Cut his throat! Cut his throat!" And I guess I'll never forget the man in black or the sight of that monster charging across the field at us.

Of course, it all began quietly enough one hot morning in July. I was still in bed when I heard my mother's voice from downstairs.

"Jimmy! For goodness sake, get up! I've called you and called you."

"O.K., Mom," I yelled back. "I'm awake now."

"Well, hurry and dress," Mom said. "Your father's finished his breakfast and I have to get ready for the Garden Club. It's after eight."

After eight! I was out of bed in one leap. I hadn't meant to sleep that late. Unless I got downstairs fast, I might miss the phone call.

I pulled on jeans and a T-shirt and made for the stairs. But just as I started down, the telephone rang. I heard my father answer it.

"Hello?" he said.

Then there was a pause.

"What's that?" My dad sounded very surprised. "Who is this anyway? . . . Hello! . . . Hello!"

I looked down the stair well. My father was standing beside the hall table directly below me. He had taken the telephone away from his ear and was staring at it in a puzzled way.

My mother came bustling out of the kitchen.

"Who was it, John?" she asked. "Was it Ann? Has anything happened?"

Ann's my seventeen-year-old sister. She was away at a girls' camp where she had a job as a counsellor.

"No . . . no," my father said. "It was either a wrong number or an imbecile's gotten loose from the mental hospital.

The person on the other end told me that the kangaroos had escaped!"

"Kangaroos!" my mother gasped. "What on earth?"

"You've got me," my dad said. "I'm just repeating what I heard."

I took a tight grip on the rail of the staircase. *The kangaroos had escaped!* It was the secret message from X.

I waited until my father put on his coat and left for the gas company where he's head accountant. Then, I raced downstairs. I was pretty excited. X didn't send a message like that unless something unusual had happened.

Mom had my breakfast all ready. She believed that everybody should eat a lot in the morning—except herself. She only had a cup of coffee and dry toast because she was trying to reduce. I went through cereal, a poached egg, and a glass of milk as quickly as possible.

When I was finished, I said, casually, "I guess I'll go out."

"All right," Mom said, sort of absent-mindedly. "Are you still trying to round up new customers?"

"Sure," I said. "But it's a tough job."

I got my bike from the shed and headed for the street. What my mother had meant by me rounding up customers had to do with my newspaper route. The *Crestwood Daily Ledger* had its yearly drive on for new subscribers. And the boy who brought in the most orders won a grand prize. They never announced what the prize would be in advance. But it was usually something pretty fancy and I wanted to win it. I was neck and neck with a kid in the south end of town and I figured that if I could sign up a couple more people I might come out ahead.

But I can tell you I wasn't thinking of the *Ledger's* contest or any grand prize as I pedaled down Maple Street. The only thing on my mind was that message from X.

X lived four blocks from me, on Chestnut Drive. For reasons of secrecy, I didn't approach his place from the front. Instead, I went along an alley that ran behind the property.

The rear end of X's garage was on this alley. It had been a coach house back in the horse-and-buggy days and was good-sized, with an upstairs. When I reached the garage, I got off my bike and pushed through the thick bushes until I was facing the north side of the building. Then, making doubly sure that I hadn't been seen, I pressed the third nail in the fourth board from the bottom.

Almost at once, a metallic voice sounded from a hidden amplifier. It wasn't loud . . . little more than a whisper.

"Your name and business?"

"Operative Three," I said. "Official business."

I waited a moment, then gave the pass words. "The sun shines but the ice is slippery."

Suddenly, a section of the garage wall slid open in front of me. I ducked through and the panel slipped back into place. It was pitch black inside until a bluish light winked on and I saw the staircase ahead.

I mounted the stairs and as I did so, they began folding up behind me with the soft clicking of well-oiled machinery. At the top, another panel opened and I stepped out into a room.

I had been in the room many times before but I always got a kick out of it. What a place! It looked like a cross between a machine shop, a research laboratory and the inside of a space ship.

There were work benches and tables and power tools and scientific apparatus—a small lathe, an electric saw and drill, racks of test tubes and bottles, a microscope . . . the works. Everything was neat and orderly but you could tell that the stuff wasn't there just for decoration.

The room seemed to be deserted until a large mirror at the far end swung silently to one side—and I saw X.

He was seated in a chair in what he called his "inner sanctum." He had on a long white coat, the kind scientists wear, and his fingers were pressed tightly together to make a church steeple. He gazed at me over them. Then he said,

"I observe that you came with great haste, Operative Three. You overslept and ate your breakfast rapidly. But a poached egg is, fortunately, quite digestible."

"Yeah, I did make it fast," I said. "But how did you know that and about the poached egg?"

He took off his glasses, polished them and smiled.

"Quite simple. Your hair is uncombed. Your sneakers don't match. You neglected to brush your teeth and wash your face. Obviously, you dressed in a rush. Futhermore, you were not on hand to answer the telephone at the appointed hour. As for the poached egg, I detect a small portion of yellow matter clinging to a corner of your mouth. It might have come from a fried egg . . . or a boiled one. But a poached egg has a subtle difference in coloration."

Of course, he'd hit everything right on the head. He always did. He was a whiz at deduction.

X was a whiz at a lot of things. He was about my age and

we were in the same class at school. But he always seemed years older. His real name was Barclay Benton. Only most of the kids called him "Brains" Benton. That was because he was so doggone smart.

Brains' father was a professor at Crestwood College and his mother was an artist. She taught at the college, too. Brains was an only child and he lived a life that every kid in town envied. I mean by that that his parents let him do a lot of things the rest of us couldn't.

For instance, he'd been given the full use of the rooms over the garage. And nobody said boo when he turned them into a crime laboratory. He'd rigged up the secret entrance I'd come through and the folding stairs, all on his own. And he'd installed the trick mirror which was normal on one side but could be seen through like glass from the other.

There were a lot more slick gadgets in the lab, too, like a hidden tape recorder to take down conversations and a burglar alarm system triggered by photoelectric cells. He had fingerprinting equipment, chemicals for analyzing clues and just about everything there was for crime detection.

If you think from this that Brains had a lot of money, you're wrong. He made most of the things himself from junk he scrounged from garages and tool shops and even from the town dump. I remember him removing the motor from an old vacuum cleaner that had been thrown out and reconditioning it for one of his inventions.

Of course, he did have an uncle in the city who sent him some things. But mostly, Brains did it all himself. If he needed money, he earned it by repairing electrical appliances for neighbors.

Brains and I got together about a year ago when we found we were both interested in crime detection. Naturally we were careful to keep our detective partnership undercover. That's why we used the terms "X" and "Operative Three."

The partnership worked out fine. Brains did most of the thinking. And I did most of the doing, like shadowing people and collecting fingerprints. In the crime lab we had a file of fingerprints from almost every kid in school. And not one of 'em knew we'd taken them. I spent months, with Brains' help, picking up the prints from drinking glasses and plastic book covers and other objects.

They say that a detective should be able to go unnoticed in a crowd. I guess that tags me pretty well. I'm about the height and weight of the average kid of my age. My hair's dark brownish, so are my eyes. My face is sort of round and I have freckles, but no more than a lot of guys.

But Brains . . . once you'd seen him, you'd never forget him. His hair was the color of . . . well, ripe strawberries is all I can think of. He had a long bony nose that he imagined was like Sherlock Holmes'. And it was. His eyes were very blue and he had great big feet. He was extra tall, too, and so thin he looked as if he might break in the middle some day. And, of course, he talked as if he were reading out of an encyclopedia.

But don't get the idea that he was any namby-pamby pushover. He was about the best pitcher our school ever had, even though he didn't like sports very much. He'd rung up four shutouts and two no-hitters in the past season. Pitching appealed to him only because it was scientific.

If I seem to have made Brains out to be a pretty extraordinary character, he was. But he was a lot of fun, too, and regular.

Well, I didn't waste any time getting down to business and asking him why he'd used the hurry-up kangaroo signal.

"For Pete's sake, what's happened, X?" I said. "Let's have the news."

"The pearls, Operative Three," he said, putting on his official deep voice. "They've found the pearls."

That was a blow. There hadn't been a crime or anything close to a crime in town for months. Then, yesterday, the *Crestwood Daily Ledger* had carried the story of the mayor's wife losing a string of valuable pearls. She'd claimed that their house had been ransacked.

"Who took 'em?" I asked.

"Nobody," Brains said. "She just mislaid them. She forgot that when she went out she had hidden them at the bottom of the laundry hamper. This morning she remembered and found them. The news was announced over the radio."

I sat down on a chair. Well, that washed out the one case we'd hoped to work on.

"Did you call me here just to tell me that?" I asked.

"Of course. I didn't want you to start investigating the case when there was no case. But more than that, I have something for you to do."

"What?" I asked eagerly.

"I want you to go out and find a mystery, Operative Three. And find one this morning. I cannot accompany you. I am busy learning how to make plaster casts of footprints."

He gestured to a book entitled *Ways and Means of Trapping the Criminal.*

"Now look," I said. "How'm I going to round up a mystery? The only mystery I know of is where to find new subscribers for the *Ledger.*"

"Perhaps," Brains said, "you will run into something while you are calling on prospects. Keep your eyes open, Operative Three. Never forget that a detective must be observant. And report to me at noon hour."

There was no sense sticking around, so I left. But I wasn't feeling too happy. Sure, find a mystery. Find subscribers. A fat chance I had of doing either.

I probably would've skipped the whole business and gone swimming if I hadn't run into Stony Rhodes downtown. Stony was the kid I figured I had to beat to win the *Ledger's* grand prize.

"Hi, Jimmy," Stony said. "Well, I guess I got you licked. I just signed up two more people."

That jolted me.

"Oh, yeah?" I said. "Who?"

"The Eatons and that new guy in the supermarket with the funny ears, Mr. Donner. And I got a third hot prospect. You might as well give in."

He let loose that silly laugh of his and rode away.

Me give in to that guy, I thought. Like heck I would.

That's when I decided to go out to the old Madden house. I'd had the place in mind all along. I knew the new people who had moved in didn't take the *Ledger.* But I'd shied away from calling on them . . . and for a good reason.

The old Madden house was supposed to be haunted.

CHAPTER 2

Hidden Eyes

THIS Madden house was a real spooky place, believe me. It was set off all by itself in a swampy section about half a mile from town. There were no neighbors within shouting distance. And I don't wonder. I wouldn't want to live near there, either.

The house had been built over a hundred years ago by a man named Noah Madden who'd made a fortune in lumber or coal or something. He must have been quite a character from all accounts, tight-fisted with his money and always afraid somebody was going to rob him. I guess that's why he put up the kind of house he did.

It was like a castle, sort of, only ugly looking, with high walls and turrets and a tower. But Mr. Madden didn't get to live there long. One night somebody broke in and gave him the business with a shotgun.

Since then the Madden place had been haunted. Or so the story went. Old-timers said that Madden's ghost prowled the house looking for the guy who'd knocked him off. And they claimed, too, that only a few of the people who rented the place after that stayed very long. And the ones who did went slab-dab crazy.

Of course, I'd no idea how true this talk was. The Madden place had been deserted for as long as I could remember—until these new tenants had taken over a month ago. And all I'd been able to find out about them was that their name was Duval and they didn't subscribe to the *Ledger*.

Well, like I said, I went out there. But I'll admit I wasn't exactly relaxed. And by the time I'd ridden my bike halfway up the lane that led to the house, I was beginning to wonder whether beating Stony Rhodes to the grand prize was such a hot idea after all.

There was no sign of life around the house. It just stood there, big and silent, as if daring me to come closer.

The building had taken a licking from the weather. Rain and winds had pitted the bricks and the wood was grayed out and rotting. A lot of the windows had been broken. Some had been boarded up but others had been left with holes in the glass.

It took about all the nerve I had to get off my bike and walk to the front door. All the while I had the shivery feeling that I was being watched by hidden eyes.

I had just raised my hand to knock when suddenly the door was yanked open—and I found myself staring at a strange-looking man.

He was bald as an egg and all bent over. But the really weird thing about him was what he was wearing. He had on a blue and white striped bathing suit—the kind men wore in the gay Nineties with pants below the knees and sleeves halfway down the arms. To top it all, he had a pair of up-to-date skin-diver's goggles over his eyes.

He gazed at me through the goggles.

"Did you bring the fish?" he asked.

"The fish!" I managed to get out. "No . . . I . . . I came to see if you would like to take the evening paper, the *Crestwood Daily Ledger.*"

"Can it be read underwater?" he asked eagerly.

Creeps! That really threw me. What had I got into anyway?

"I don't know," I said. "But it's a good paper. You'll like it. I'll deliver it every afternoon."

For the first time I noticed that the man held a big sea shell in his hand. He now put it to his ear. I began to edge away.

"Wait," he said. "I will have to ask Gustav."

He was gone in a flash and the door closed. I stood there, wondering whether I should beat it while the beating was good or wait for this guy, Gustav, whoever he was.

Before I could make up my mind, the door opened again and a fat man appeared. He had a beard and a mustache and he was smoking a pipe with a tremendous bowl. He had on strange clothes, too, the kind you see in pictures of German beer gardens . . . short pants, stockings to his knees and a little jacket with decorations on it. He had one of those funny hats on his head with a thing like a shaving brush up one side.

"Montgomery tells me dot you zell noosepapers," he said. His accent seemed German to me. "*Ja?*"

"Yes, sir," I said. "I'm taking subscriptions to the . . ."

"I do not like noosepapers," he said, cutting me off. "They tell lies."

"Not the *Ledger*, sir," I said. "It's one of the best papers in the state. Truthful, up-to-the-minute news coverage, both local and international."

Once I got started I let him have the full sales pitch. I told him about the columns by famous reporters, the woman's page and the sports section. I explained how much the paper would cost him per week and when it would be delivered. I even went into the business of the contest and my ambition to win the grand prize.

He listened, pulling at his big pipe and muttering, "*Ja . . . ja . . . ja.*"

Then, as a clincher, I ended up with, "And the *Ledger* carries the best comic strips for your child."

This seemed to have a strange effect on him. He lowered his pipe and glared at me.

"Child?" he said. "What do you mean—child? I have no child."

With that he stepped back and the door closed with a bang.

Well, I lost no time leaving. I'd done my best but I'd rung up a big *no sale*.

I had just got on my bike when I glanced back at the house—and I almost flipped at what I saw.

The curtains at one of the ground floor windows had been pulled aside. And there, clear as anything, I saw a boy of my own age looking out.

Then, the boy vanished and the curtains came together again. It was as if somebody had quickly yanked the kid out of sight.

CHAPTER 3

Scream in the Night

ONLY a rocket could have gone down the lane to the road faster than I did. And I didn't slow up until I reached the garage back of Brains' house. I'd flopped in getting a new subscriber to the *Ledger* but I'd sure run into one lulu of a mystery.

Brains was in the middle of a footprint experiment when I came charging into the crime lab. He had one shoe off and was pressing his bare foot into a box filled with earth. Beside him was a bowl of freshly mixed plaster to be used in making a cast of the footprint.

He was mad as a hornet at me breaking in on his work.

But he snapped out of it when I rattled off what had happened.

"Aha!" he exclaimed. "You have indeed discovered something most suspicious, Operative Three."

"Suspicious!" I said. "It's an out and out kidnapping. That boy I saw is being held for ransom by those two maniacs."

"A possibility," Brains said. "Did he signal you for help?"

"No. But he probably hadn't time before somebody pulled him away from the window."

Brains lifted his bare foot from the box of earth and began to pace up and down the lab, hands clasped behind his back, in that master-detective way he had.

"Give me a full description of these two men—the one known as Montgomery and the Germanic person called Gustav. Try to remember every detail, Operative Three."

That wasn't hard. The picture I had in my mind of those two characters was as vivid as a 3-D, big screen job done in full color.

"They're both as nutty as a batch of almond cookies," I ended up.

"Perhaps," Brains muttered.

"Perhaps—nothing," I said. "Why would they go around dressed like that if they weren't off their rockers? Hey, maybe the stories about the Madden house are true and living there has made them wacky."

"They may well be unbalanced mentally," Brains said. "But I rather believe that it was an act to make you think they were insane."

"Huh?" I gasped. "Why would they pull a stunt like that?"

"The reason is elementary. They did it to scare you off. To make sure you would never return to the house."

See what I mean by Brains being smart? Me, I would never have figured it that way. But it made sense. Those getups that Montgomery and Gustav had worn were just a little too zany.

Brains was staring into space and I knew from past experience that his mind had slipped into high gear.

"These men you encountered are no ordinary criminals," he said. "They show rare imagination and cunning. They are the type that can become most vicious when cornered. We will have to proceed with great caution."

I began to feel a little less enthusiastic about the case.

"Look, X," I said. "Maybe we should report this to the police."

Brains wheeled around so quickly he knocked over the bowl of plaster. He didn't seem to notice.

"This is our case and we will conduct our own investigation," he said severely. "If it should prove too difficult for us to handle, then and *only* then will the law enforcement officers be notified. What are we, detectives—or mice?"

I wet my lips. "O.K. . . . O.K.," I said. "So what do we do?"

"Proceed to the scene of the crime, of course."

"You mean . . . go out there to . . . to the Madden house?"

"Naturally," Brains said.

He looked cautiously to left and right as if making sure no one had sneaked into the lab. Then, lowering his voice, he went on, "Now listen to me, Operative Three. Seal your lips. Tell no one what you have seen. Then, tonight, when the sun has sunk below the horizon and the shadows of evening are thickening, we will stalk the Madden residence. Do you understand?"

"Yeah," I said when I was finally able to make my lips work. "But I'll have to deliver my papers first and have dinner."

"Ample time for that if you move with dispatch. Meet me here at seven-thirty on the dot. Do not be late."

As it turned out, I was late. First, something happened to the *Ledger's* presses and there was a delay in getting the bundles of papers to us carriers. Then, I ran into trouble with that crabby Mr. Thomas over on Lilac Boulevard.

I'm a dead shot with a folded newspaper. I can toss an edition of the *Ledger* from the street and make it plop right on a welcome mat. But my aim was sour when I got to Mr. Thomas' house. Maybe I was hurrying too much. Anyway, the paper landed on the roof of his porch and he made me stop and climb up and get it.

To top it all, my mother met my dad downtown after work to help him buy a suit. They didn't get home for ages. And of course, we had to have one of those dinners that takes forever to cook.

I didn't have any trouble getting permission to go over to Brains' when we were finished eating. My parents were used to that. But it was close to eight o'clock when I reached the lab.

Brains didn't say much but it was plain from the way he glared at his watch that he was put out. He was loaded down with equipment. He had a coil of rope looped around his middle and hanging from his belt were a hatchet, a hunting knife and a camera. A canvas kit bag was slung over one shoulder. It seemed already filled but he shoved in a flashlight, a magnifying glass, a tape measure and binoculars.

"Come along," he said abruptly. "We won't have too much daylight left."

We didn't go on our bikes. Instead, we hoofed it, sticking to back alleys and side streets until we were clear of town. Then we headed cross-country for the big patch of woods behind the Madden place. Brains led the way, walking so fast with those long legs of his that I was forced to break into a trot to keep up.

Once we entered the woods he slowed down. He had to. It was like a jungle in there with heavy underbrush and thickets and vines trailing all over the place. It was gloomy, too, and full of dark shadows where somebody could be crouched, ready to jump out at you.

We were safe enough from being seen from the Madden house while we were in the woods. But what worried me was how we were going to cross the field that lay between the woods and the house. There was little shelter in that field except for tall grass and weeds and some rocks. As for Brains being satisfied with a long distance view from the edge of the woods, I knew better than *that*.

Of course, I should have realized that he'd have a plan figured out in advance. And he did.

We had worked our way almost to the other side of the woods when Brains called a halt. He lowered his kit bag and took from it, of all things, two pairs of old pajamas. The pajama coats and pants looked as if somebody had used them for paint rags. They were covered all over with dabs and smears of color—yellowish-green, brown and red and streaks of black and purple.

"Creeps!" I said. "What's the big idea?"

"Our stalking suits," Brains said. There was a note of pride in his voice. "I fixed them this afternoon. The colors will blend with the background and help camouflage our movements. We should be able to maneuver right up to the house. Put one on. Hurry now."

He began pulling one of the suits over his clothes and I did the same with the other. It was a neat idea, I had to admit. But just getting into an outfit like that made the danger ahead seem much more real.

Brains had also brought along two battered felt hats. I guess they'd belonged to his father. Crouched down, he decorated them with twigs and leaves and grass, shoving the greenery into the hat bands and through holes in the crowns. When he was finished the hats were completely covered and we put them on.

As a final touch he took a piece of burnt cork from his bag and we blackened our faces.

Brains leaned back and gave me a quick once-over.

"Excellent," he said. "You have the appearance of a badly tended grave, Operative Three."

I winced. "Don't say things like that," I told him.

He was rearranging his gear and I doubt if he even heard me.

"From now on we must exercise extreme caution," he said. "Follow me."

At the edge of the woods we stopped again, lying flat.

"There it is," Brains whispered. "The house of mystery."

He didn't have to tell me. The sun had set but there was plenty of light for me to see the Madden place on the far side of the field. It seemed even uglier from the rear than from the front. There were a number of run-down buildings at the back—a barn and a shed and something that might have once been a chicken house. Only the roof had caved in and so had one wall. Nearby the framework of a windmill stuck up into the sky. The breeze was turning its few remaining vanes and the windmill was creaking and wheezing as if in pain. It wasn't a pleasant sound.

Brains took out his binoculars and studied the place. "See anyone?" I asked.

He shook his head.

"Maybe they've gone away," I said hopefully. "Maybe they got scared I'd caught sight of the boy and they beat it."

"No," Brains said. "Somebody's there."

"How do you know?"

"That laundry didn't attach itself to that line."

I hadn't noticed the washing hung on a clothesline by the back door. But now I did. It was in plain sight and seemed to be mainly sheets and towels.

Brains sort of got your goat at times. I mean the big-headed way he talked as if he were actually Sherlock Holmes or somebody. I'd always wanted to take him down a peg and this seemed to be my chance.

"The wash could've been put out hours ago," I said scornfully. "And left there."

"Nothing of the sort," Brains said. "The articles were arranged on the clothesline within the last fifteen minutes."

I was sure I had him now. He was just guessing.

"And how do you figure that?" I asked.

"It's obvious," he said. "The sheets and towels hang straight down and are not blown by the breeze. Clearly, they are wet. And if they are wet in hot weather like this, someone must have pegged them to the line very recently."

Well, I knew when I was licked. He'd hit the bull's-eye dead center, as usual.

"That's neat figuring," I admitted. And it sure was.

Brains shrugged. "Commonplace. Simple observation and basic deduction."

He slipped his binoculars back into his kit bag and began to gather his legs under him.

"Those desperados are apparently inside the house," he said. "This is our chance. Remember, keep your body flat. And don't raise your head whatever you do. If they see us, it might be fatal."

With those comforting words he slid forward into the field and began crawling like a snake through the tall grass and weeds. I took a deep breath, all the way down to my toes. Then, I followed.

I don't know the measurements of that field. Maybe it was two hundred yards long. But it felt like two thousand to me as I wriggled across the uneven ground. I couldn't get out of my mind the thought that at any moment one of those thugs might let loose with a rifle from an upper window.

Was I scared? Well, either my teeth were chattering or somebody was practicing with castanets.

I didn't catch up with Brains until he stopped behind a

big boulder that jutted out of the ground a short distance from the barn.

"You aren't going any nearer, are you?" I whispered.

"Of course *we* are," Brains said. "That barn will provide an excellent observation post. Quickly now."

He was on his way once more. I didn't want to be left alone. So I went along.

We had covered about half the distance to the barn when it happened. There was no warning. Suddenly a terrible shriek came from the house. And a voice screamed, "Cut his throat! Cut his throat!"

CHAPTER 4

The Man in Black

THEY say that people have died of fright. And I guess I came close to being one of them. I just lay there, hugging the ground. Then I did the only thing I could think of. I ran.

I had sense enough to keep bent over, but that didn't slow me down. All I wanted was to get away from there—fast. And, believe it or not, Brains was doing the same thing. In fact, he tore back across the field at such a clip that he hit the woods two leaps ahead of me. We didn't stop until we were halfway to the other side.

It was Brains who put on the brakes first.

"Confound it!" he said when he was able to get his breath. "Fine detectives we turned out to be, stampeding like scared rabbits."

He was scowling and looked mad.

"What did you want us to do?" I asked. "Hang around and get our throats cut, too? Not me, brother."

"We have no proof that anyone's throat was cut," he said. "We just jumped to conclusions and panicked. I'm ashamed of myself."

"You heard that yell," I said. "They've murdered that poor kid."

"The yell could have come from a television set or a radio. Or they might have seen us and done it to scare us away."

"Baloney," I said. "You can't make me believe that."

Brains took off his stalking hat and ran his fingers through his red hair.

"The odd thing is that the voice most certainly wasn't a man's," he said thoughtfully. "Far too shrill. It didn't sound like a woman's, either. It had a strange inhuman quality to it."

"You mean it . . . it might have been old Noah Madden's ghost?" I said.

"I don't know what I mean," Brains said. "Frankly, Operative Three, I am in a quandary. In other words, I am puzzled."

"Well, let the cops figure it out. They're good at puzzles." I was anxious to be on our way. "Come on. We've got to get to a phone and call them."

But Brains had other ideas.

"I suggest that we do not notify the police," he said.

"What!" I gasped.

"At least not until we have done some more investigating on our own and are certain a crime has been committed."

He glanced over his shoulder.

"Perhaps we should go back right now."

Just the thought of returning to that awful old house gave me the willies. It was dark in the woods and getting darker.

"Are you nuts?" I said. "It's late. We're due home."

"Well, you may be right," he said. "Our parents might get disturbed and start asking questions. It is essential that we keep them in ignorance of our crime detection activities. We will therefore postpone further observations until morning."

That was a laugh. As if anybody could make me do this thing all over again.

But at ten a.m. the next day, guess where I was. Yeah, lying flat on my stomach and staring through a clump of high grass at the Madden house.

Oh, sure, I'd argued with Brains all the way home. I'd pointed out that it was the duty of every citizen to report a crime and not take the law into his own hands. I'd stated that it was plain suicide to go snooping around the Madden place again and that I wasn't having any part of it.

But I might as well have been sounding off to a slightly deaf penguin at the South Pole for all the good it did. And in the end you can see who got his way. Certainly not Jimmy Carson, otherwise known as Operative Three.

Yet everything looked different that morning. The sun was shining, the sky was blue and I could hear a meadowlark singing not too far away. Even the old house didn't seem quite so gloomy and scary.

We'd put on our stalking suits again but we'd picked a different spot for our spying. It was in the field but a little to the east of the house, back of a rise of ground. Being broad daylight, Brains had thought it might be smart not to go too close. Now that was something I agreed with.

Well, we hadn't been there two minutes when we heard the back door of the house bang, and a dog started barking. By shifting my position a little I was able to see that two people had left the house. With them was a small spotted dog. One of the people was a short, roundish man, maybe forty-five or fifty. The other was a boy.

And get this. The boy was carrying an umbrella—the small kind called a parasol that ladies sometimes use. He had it open and there wasn't a cloud in the sky.

"Brains!" I said. "I think it's the kid I saw at the window. Give me the glasses, quick!"

Brains handed over his binoculars and I put them to my eyes. It was the kid, all right. I was sure now, seeing him close up. I remembered how blond his hair had been, almost white—just like this one's.

"They didn't kill him after all," I said. "He's alive!"

"If he isn't, he's putting on a fine act," Brains said. "How about that man with him. Is he Montgomery or Gustav?"

"He doesn't look like either of them," I said.

Brains grunted. I could see he was sort of disturbed that there might be a third man at the house. But what threw me was the sight of that boy holding an umbrella when the sun was shining.

"The kid must be batty," I said to Brains. "Like those other two."

Then something happened that really floored us both.

The washing that had been hung out the night before had been taken in and the clothesline was empty. The line was stretched tight as a drum between two posts. The line wasn't rope. It was wire. You could see its silvery shine in the sunlight. Propped up next to one of the posts was a stepladder.

Well, what did this kid do but climb up the ladder and walk out on the wire line! Yeah, walk right out on it, standing up. And he didn't go just a few steps. Putting one foot in front of the other, and holding the umbrella in his right hand, he went clear across to the other side.

All the while the roundish man kept pace with him on the ground, as if ready to catch him if he fell.

"A tightrope walker!" Brains exclaimed.

If the kid had turned into a green-skinned Martian with four eyes, I couldn't have been more surprised. A tightrope walker! So that was why he had the umbrella—for balance.

When he reached the other end of the wire, the boy swung around and came back. He did it as easily as if he were drifting into Bennett's Drug Store for a chocolate malted.

Brains turned his head as if to say something to me. But instead of speaking, he looked past me and the darndest expression come over his face.

"Don't move," he hissed.

"What's wrong?" I whispered.

"Over there. Back of those bushes."

I looked around cautiously. At first I didn't see anything out of the ordinary. Then I saw plenty.

Less than half a city block away was a man. He was crouched down behind a clump of laurel. He had on a black shirt and black pants. Even his hat was black. I couldn't see much of his face because he was holding binoculars to his eyes. He wasn't looking in our direction. He had the glasses aimed at the back yard where the boy was walking the wire.

"Creeps!" I whispered.

"So we aren't the only ones who have the Madden house under observation," Brains said.

He had moved close to me so that his lips were right at my ear.

"Maybe he's a G-man," I said. "Or a foreign spy."

"He could be anything," Brains whispered. "He apparently has not seen us. His sole interest seems to be in the activities at the house."

How the guy had got there, I couldn't tell, of course. But he had probably sneaked out of the woods, just as we had, only from another direction.

Everything sure had got mixed up. The boy turning out to be alive and a hot-shot on a tightrope, and now this mysterious man muscling into the act. But it was nothing to what happened next.

I had just taken a look back at the Madden yard when the boy ended his trick stuff by jumping off the wire. And he didn't just jump. Tossing the umbrella aside, he gave a leap into the air and turned a complete somersault before landing on his feet on the ground.

"Whew!" I said. "Get a load of that!"

"Shhhh!" Brains warned.

He had raised himself up a little to get a better view.

"I believe we are about to have developments," he whispered.

And did we ever.

The roundish man slapped the kid on the back as if he was pleased with what the boy had done. Then, the man walked away toward the barn. The kid didn't go with him. Instead he called to a little dog who'd been sniffing and exploring around. Then, the boy and the dog left the yard and started coming across the field in our direction.

"Down!" Brains whispered.

I burrowed as low as I could in the grass. Even so I could see pretty well what was going on.

The boy picked up a stick and threw it far off to one side, away from where we were. The dog went chasing after it, barking. In a minute the dog was back, the stick in his mouth. The kid took the stick and threw it again.

The two of them kept on playing this game. And all the time the boy was walking nearer and nearer, through the waist-high weeds and grass. He'd changed his direction slightly and I realized he was going to pass very close to where the man in black was hiding.

It was pretty tense, I tell you, just waiting and wondering what would happen.

"The dog's liable to get our scent or the stranger's," I whispered to Brains.

"No," Brains whispered back. "We're both downwind."

Well, that's the way it went until the kid was almost at

the clump of laurel bushes. Then, just as he was about to pass the far side of the bushes, he stopped and gave the stick an extra long heave. The dog went bouncing off in pursuit.

I heard Brains' sudden intake of breath. And then I saw the reason.

The man in black was rising slowly to his feet. In one hand he had what seemed to be a canvas bag. It was the size of a potato sack. In the other hand he was gripping something short and thick.

Brains was using the binoculars again.

"He's got a blackjack," Brains whispered. "He's going to attack the boy."

There seemed no doubt about that. The man was now slithering around the bushes toward the kid whose back was to him.

Brains grabbed me by the arm.

"We can't let this happen," he said. "Come on, Jimmy."

The fact that Brains called me Jimmy and not Operative Three will show you how excited he was.

Brains eased himself up and so did I. Then, all crouched over, the two of us left our spying post and started across the field. We tried to move quietly, but we didn't waste time.

I guess if anyone had been watching, the whole thing might have looked almost funny. There was the boy standing with his back turned, watching the dog hunt for the stick, not knowing that a man with a blackjack was sneaking up behind him. And the man didn't know that Brains and I were sneaking up on *him*.

But it wasn't funny to me. My heart was hammering so hard I thought it would kick a hole clear through my chest. At any second, I expected the man to hear us and turn around.

Thank goodness, he didn't. He kept on slowly creeping nearer and nearer to the kid. He must have figured that he wouldn't need the blackjack because he let it dangle from a cord around his wrist and used both hands to grip the top of the sack. He held the top open and it was plain to see that he planned to pull the sack down over the boy's head and shoulders to smother any yell and to pin the kid's arms to his sides.

Brains and I had almost made it to the bushes when, all of a sudden, the man raised the sack and yanked it over the boy's head.

"Charge!" Brains whispered.

We did.

I've played a lot of football, so I let go with a flying tackle. I hit the man just below the knees. At the same time, Brains gave a leap and grabbed the guy around the neck.

We must have slammed into him plenty hard for he went down *whammo*, right on top of the boy. And Brains and I ended up draped across the man.

Then, everything went slightly haywire. The bag was over the boy's head and the upper part of his body. He was thrashing around and making muffled noises and trying to squirm out from under the man. And the man was snarling a lot of foreign words and fighting and kicking to get free of us.

He gave a terrific heave and brought his arm back. His

elbow caught me in the stomach. Before I knew it, I was sent flying. I must have hit my head on a rock or something, because when I landed the whole world exploded in a burst of stars.

I couldn't have been out long. Yet, when I opened my eyes, plenty had happened. Brains was tugging the sack off the kid and the kid's attacker was running like crazy across the field. And yipping and snapping at his heels was the little spotted dog. A moment later, the two of them disappeared into the woods.

I don't know what made me look in the direction of the Madden house. But when I did, I figured I'd really been knocked groggy.

The roundish, middle-aged man was coming from the back yard of the house. But he wasn't running or walking. He was riding, so help me, *an elephant!*

CHAPTER 5

The Chase

I CLOSED my eyes and opened them again. But that didn't change anything. The elephant was still there. And so was the man on its back.

It wasn't one of those giant elephants. It was smallish and gray, with flappy ears. It was heading for us in a sort of lurching gallop, swaying from side to side.

I guess Brains had been too busy freeing the boy to notice what was coming our way. And the kid certainly hadn't had much of a chance to see anything except the inside of a sack.

Just then, the elephant raised its trunk and trumpeted.

I think that's what you call it. Anyway, it's an awful noise —like something made by a cracked bugle.

Brains jumped as if he'd sat on a cactus. He whirled around and his mouth dropped open. For once in his life he hadn't a word to say.

But the boy was different. The moment he caught sight of the elephant and its rider he started racing to meet them.

"Bimbo!" he hollered.

The roundish man waved a short pole he held in one hand.

"I'm coming, Skeets!" he shouted back.

"Somebody jumped me and threw a bag over my head," the boy called Skeets yelled. "Then these two guys showed up."

Bimbo—I figured that must be the roundish man's name— kept the elephant at full speed. "I saw what happened," Bimbo shouted. "Get aboard. We're going after him."

As the elephant thundered past, Bimbo leaned down. He grabbed Skeets by a hand. At the same moment, the boy gave a leap and, quick as a flash, he was up on the elephant's back behind Bimbo. You never saw anything like it. Real circus stuff.

"Was it Otto who tried to grab me?" I heard Skeets ask. "Was it Otto, Bimbo?"

He sounded scared.

"I don't think so," Bimbo yelled back over his shoulder. "Too tall. But we'll soon find out."

He prodded the elephant with the end of the pole.

"Faster, Marjory!" he bellowed. "Faster!"

Then they were out of earshot as the elephant pounded

on toward the woods, shaking the field under our feet.

I think I would have left well enough alone. But not Brains. He didn't dilly-dally around. Instead, he went after the elephant as if he were trying to catch a train.

"They may need help!" he shouted to me. "Come on!"

Well, of course, old Operative Three did.

Now if you think an elephant can't run fast, you should have been chasing this monster known as Marjory. She was across the field in nothing flat, leaving us far behind. And she didn't slow down when she hit the woods. She went through it like a runaway Army tank. I don't know how Bimbo and Skeets stayed on her back. But they did.

From far ahead I could hear the little dog barking. It was a sure tip-off to where the man in black had gone.

But nobody caught him. When Brains and I came panting out on the dirt road at the far side of the woods, the elephant had stopped and Bimbo and Skeets had climbed to the ground. The little dog was there, too. And, in the distance, a car was disappearing down the road.

The man in black had got away. But he'd left something behind. The little dog had it in his mouth. It was a piece of the man's pants—the part he sat on.

I flopped down at the side of the road to catch my breath and try to figure things out. But my mind was whirling as if somebody had dipped it in a rotary beater. Talk about nightmares! Brains and I had walked into the great grand-daddy of them all.

Sure we knew that Skeets hadn't been kidnapped as we'd first thought. And we knew that Bimbo wasn't a crook—

or at least he didn't seem to be. But there was plenty we *didn't* know.

Who were Bimbo and Skeets anyway? Why were they living in the old Madden house? And why did they have, of all things, an elephant? And how about those two crazy guys, Montgomery and Gustav? And who was the man in black? Why had he tried to grab Skeets? And why was Skeets so scared of somebody named Otto? And above all, who had screamed, "Cut his throat! Cut his throat!" And why?

See what I mean? Why? Why? Why? What? What? What? Who? Who? Who? Hundreds of 'em.

Bimbo and Skeets were standing close together, talking quietly. They looked worried. Marjory had moved to the side of the road and was calmly pulling up tufts of wild grass with her trunk and stuffing them into her mouth. The little dog just sat on his haunches, the piece of pants still in his mouth.

Brains wandered around, staring at the ground and muttering to himself. After a while he joined me.

"What do we do now?" I whispered.

"We wait," Brains said, darkly. "It's their move."

So we waited. I was glad of the chance to try my hand at Brains' trick of observation and deduction.

This Skeets was maybe a little younger than I was, but not much. He was wearing a checkered sport shirt, a pair of orange pants and rubber-soled shoes. The only thing different about him from most kids was his almost white hair. His eyebrows were the same color, too. I placed him as a regular guy who'd be great at sports.

As for Bimbo, well he was real funny looking—in a nice way, I mean. Short and fattish with a big full face and a bald head and a wide mouth. He was pretty old, close to fifty, anyway. He was wearing tan slacks and a dark blue shirt and sneakers. There was a hole in one of the sneakers and his big toe stuck out. He gave you the feeling that he could tell jokes and keep you laughing.

But he sure wasn't telling any jokes now. And Skeets wasn't doing any laughing, either.

They kept on yakking away to each other for a minute or so more. Then they turned toward us.

"Well, boys," Bimbo said, "as you can see our man made a getaway. But if it hadn't been for you two fellows, he would have taken Skeets here with him. I'm sorry I wasn't any help. I had just got Marjory out of the barn for her exercise when I saw what was happening. I want to thank you both for what you did."

"So do I," Skeets said.

He came to us and shook Brains' hand and then mine.

"Thanks," Skeets said.

"A pleasure," Brains replied. "Strictly in the line of duty."

I didn't know quite what to say so I just muttered, "Strictly in the line of duty."

Bimbo acted a little puzzled.

"There's one thing I'd like to find out," he said. "How did you boys happen to be on the spot?"

He didn't say anything about our clothes. But I could tell he was wondering how come we were dressed like a couple of AWOL Commandos.

Brains spoke up immediately.

"First," he said, in his deep voice, "may I present our credentials."

He whipped out one of our business cards like a magician producing a rabbit and handed it to Bimbo. The little man took the card and held it at arm's length, the way older people do who have forgotten their reading glasses.

Heck, I could have told him what was on the card. Brains had printed them himself on the press he'd rigged up. But we'd had an argument over what was to go on them. Finally we'd agreed and the card read like this:

THE BENTON AND CARSON
INTERNATIONAL DETECTIVE AGENCY

Confidential Investigators and Criminologists
Modern scientific methods and devices used

SHADOWING	FREE CONSULTATION
TRACING OF MISSING PERSONS	24-HOUR SERVICE
President:	*Secretary-Treasurer:*
Barclay "Brains" Benton	James "Jimmy" Carson

Skeets read the card over Bimbo's shoulder.

"You're *detectives!*" he exclaimed. "Gee!"

"Detectives or private investigators, as you will," Brains said.

Skeets was now staring hard at me and I got a little uncomfortable.

"I've seen you somewhere before," Skeets said. Then his eyes widened a bit. "Saaay! Aren't you the guy who came to the house to sell us the newspaper?"

I was surprised that he'd recognized me, especially with the burnt cork on my face.

"That's right," I said. "I talked to a man named Montgomery and to someone else called Gustav."

I noticed a look pass between Bimbo and Skeets—a sort of guarded, private look. I had the feeling that Bimbo was sending Skeets a warning of some kind.

If Brains saw the look, he paid no attention to it.

"It was my partner's call at your house," Brains said, "that awakened the interest of the Benton and Carson International Detective Agency."

And then and there, Brains launched into a full account of our investigation. He went over the whole business from our first approach to the house and that awful scream, to the attack on Skeets by the man in black.

Bimbo and Skeets didn't interrupt him. They just listened. But I must say they appeared amazed, especially Bimbo.

"And that, sir," Brains said finally, "will answer your question of how we happened to be close at hand when the assault took place."

"I see . . . I see," Bimbo muttered. "I don't wonder you were mystified by what went on at the house. Well, I can tell you this. We did want to keep people away. And for a good reason."

I edged forward, hoping he'd spill the works. But instead he changed the subject.

"Did either of you get a good look at the man who attacked Skeets?" Bimbo asked sharply. "Could you describe him? It's *very* important."

I shook my head. "I didn't see his face. All I can tell you is he wore a black hat and a black jacket and black pants."

"How about you?" Bimbo asked Brains.

"I had no opportunity to view his face, either," Brains said.

Bimbo and Skeets looked disappointed.

"However," Brains went on, "I believe I can tell you something about this person."

"What?" Bimbo asked.

"Well, he is approximately six feet tall," Brains said. "He has a minor deformity in his left foot causing him to toe in and limp slightly. At one time he was a sailor. At another time, a boxer. He is of foreign extraction and he smokes cigars."

I thought Bimbo was going to have a stroke, he got so red in the face. And Skeets' eyes darn near popped out of his head.

"Now wait a minute," Bimbo said. "You claim you don't know this man?"

"Never saw him before in my life," Brains said.

"Then how in thunder can you give such a description? Tell me that!"

Brains shrugged. "It's all very simple," he said in that superior way he has. "Just observation and deduction. For instance, I judged his height by looking at him. As for his odd manner of walking, I saw examples of his footprints in the damp soil over there. He obviously puts more weight on his right foot, and his left foot angles inward. Clearly, he is a trifle lame."

"All right," Bimbo said. He sort of growled out the words. "I'll go along with that. But what about this business of him once being a sailor and a fighter?"

"Quite elementary," Brains said. "While grappling with this person, I observed that the back of one of his hands had been tattooed with an anchor design. This suggested that he had been a seaman. I assumed that he had also been a fighter when I observed his misshapen ears. Cauliflower, I believe, is the term."

"But what about him being foreign?" Skeets asked. "And what about him smoking cigars?"

"During our tussle in the field," Brains said, "the creature exclaimed several words in a language that was not English. And as for the other matter—his clothing reeked of the distinctive odor of cigar smoke."

"It's the Joker!" Skeets let out. "Bimbo! It must have been the Joker."

Bimbo wet his lips with the tip of his tongue. Some of the color had gone from his face.

"A perfect description of him, all right," he said.

"It couldn't be anybody else!" Skeets said. "Otto sent him. They've tracked me down! The Joker will tell Otto where I am. Then he'll . . . What are we going to do, Bimbo?"

The kid was scared out of his wits.

Bimbo was plenty upset, too. You could tell from the way he kept clenching and unclenching his hands.

"We'd better get back to the house—fast!" he said. "There's no telling where Otto is. He mightn't be too far away."

Bimbo moved quickly across the road to where the elephant was feeding. He tapped the animal on one side of the trunk with the pole. Marjory stopped pulling up the grass. She slowly turned around and then began to lumber back through the woods, following the trail she had blazed.

"Home, Gulliver," Bimbo said to the little dog.

It was the first time I'd heard the dog's name.

Bimbo bent over a little bit and right away the dog jumped on his shoulders. From there, Gulliver gave a leap and landed on the elephant's back. He scampered along it until he reached Marjory's head. Then he lay down between the elephant's two flappy ears. He seemed perfectly happy riding there.

I was still gawking when I heard Bimbo speak to Brains.

"You two boys better come along," he said. "It looks as if you're in this thing whether you like it or not. But I must swear you to secrecy on everything I'm going to tell you."

"All information is treated with the strictest confidence," Brains said. "Pray proceed."

Then, as we followed the waddling elephant and her dog rider through the woods, Bimbo began to talk. It was a strange story he told. The more I heard, the faster my heart pounded. And I began to wonder if the first case of the Benton and Carson International Detective Agency mightn't turn out to be its last one, too.

CHAPTER 6

The Secret Paper

BRAINS was furious that we hadn't brought along the portable tape recorder he'd invented so we could get down Bimbo's story word for word. But I can give you the account right out of my head. I don't think I'll ever forget any of it.

The whole mysterious business, Bimbo told us, was centered around Skeets. Skeets' real name was George Skelly Fenton and he was in trouble right up to his neck. Terrible trouble.

"You see," Bimbo said, "Skeets' father and mother were famous circus performers—the world's greatest trapeze artists in their day. They were top billed as The Flying

54

Fentons. That was because of the hair-raising stunts they put on way up near the peak of the tent."

Mr. and Mrs. Fenton had come from England many years ago, Bimbo explained, and almost right away they'd hit big time. Things went so well that they soon had a circus of their own.

Skeets was a real circus kid. He'd been born and raised under the Big Top. Almost since he could stand up, he'd been taught to swing from a trapeze and walk a wire. Low down, of course, not the high stuff. That was why he'd been so good on the clothesline.

One day, when Skeets was four or five, a cousin of his father's showed up. His name was Otto Gruber. He was broke and hungry so Skeets' father gave him a job. This was Mr. Fenton's big mistake.

Otto, from what Bimbo said, was a pretty slippery character. And little by little he began to worm his way into better jobs with the Fenton circus. It wasn't long before he was in charge of the box office and was handling the money end of things.

Skeets' father was no businessman. He was only interested in giving the audiences a good show. And he didn't get wise to what was happening until it was almost too late.

According to Bimbo, Otto had been stealing money from the circus and covering up his crooked stuff by faking the books. He took so much that the circus got into a financial jam. It looked as if Skeets' father and mother would have to close down. Then, what did Otto do but offer to put up enough money to keep the circus going. It was the Fentons'

money, really. In exchange, Otto was to have part owner-
ship of the circus.

"Alf Fenton was in such a bad spot he had to agree,"
Bimbo said. "He knew that Otto was a crook. But he had no
proof."

Well, things went along like that for awhile with Otto
as a partner. But Mr. Fenton was worried. He was afraid
that Otto wouldn't be satisfied with being just a part owner
but might do something really desperate to get complete
control of the circus. He thought that Otto might even try
to kill him.

It seems that about this time, Skeets' dad got hold of
some information about Otto that Otto didn't want known.
Mr. Fenton wrote down the information on a paper. Then
he told Otto that if he tried to pull anything, the paper
would be shown to the police.

"I was probably Alf Fenton's best friend," Bimbo said.
"I was a clown and I'd been with the Fenton circus since
it started. Skeets' father always talked things over with me.
One night he called me into his office and told me about getting this dope on Otto. He didn't say what it was but I
gathered that if it ever came out, Otto would really be in
trouble."

Bimbo paused for a moment, then went on. "Alf Fenton
made me promise to take the paper to the police if anything should happen to him. He said that he was going to
put the paper in a secret place and as soon as he had, he'd
tell me where it was hidden. But he never got to tell me."

At this point, Bimbo's voice trailed off and he looked over
at Skeets. We were almost through the woods and I could

see the old Madden house in the distance across the field.

"Go on, Bimbo," Skeets said.

He seemed choked up and had a hard time getting the words out. Then he started walking quickly, moving on ahead of us as if he didn't want to hear what was coming next.

I wondered why—until Bimbo spoke again.

"Well," Bimbo said with a sort of sigh, "the reason Skeets' father didn't tell me was that the very next morning he and Skeets' mother were killed in an automobile accident."

Nobody said anything for quite a while and the only sound came from the crashing of underbrush under Marjory's big feet.

"It *was* an accident?" Brains finally asked.

Bimbo raised his shoulders and lowered them.

"It looked that way and that's how the state police put it down. I didn't say anything to Skeets at the time, but I had my doubts. I started hunting for the secret paper right away. But I couldn't find it anywhere. I didn't have much time to look, though. For with Alf Fenton gone, the first thing Otto did was fire me and my wife. She was the fortuneteller and mind reader in the circus. In fact, Otto got rid of everybody who'd been friends of the Fentons and brought in his own cronies like the Joker."

It must have been awful for poor Skeets, losing his parents like that and then not having Bimbo or any friends around, either.

"Of course Skeets had inherited his father's interest in the circus," Bimbo said. "That made him Otto's partner.

But because Skeets was a minor, Otto took complete charge of the management of the business."

"Couldn't Skeets have objected even if he was under age?" Brains asked.

"I suppose so," Bimbo said. "And he might have. He'd never liked Otto. And he felt Otto had never liked him. But Otto played it smart. He began being very palsy-walsy. He told Skeets that he'd look after everything and that he'd do his best to be a father to him. He even suggested becoming Skeets' legal guardian. Skeets was so dazed from the shock of losing his parents that he agreed and Otto had the official papers put through. That placed Otto right in the driver's seat."

The circus was on tour at this time, playing one town after another, and Skeets tried to get used to his new life. Then something upsetting happened. One afternoon Skeets found that somebody had searched his room on the circus train. Everything he owned had been gone through, especially the contents of a trunk his parents had left him. The stuff had been put back in place but Skeets wasn't fooled. What puzzled him was that nothing was missing.

A few days later, when Skeets returned to his room unexpectedly, he found Otto there. Otto made some excuse about looking for a piece of costume. But Skeets didn't believe him.

From then on, Otto's gentle handling of Skeets was over. He got very tough with him. He made Skeets practice hour after hour on the trapeze and try stunts that were far too hard for a kid to do. And he forced Skeets to work up high near the top of the tent. Skeets was good but not that good, and a couple of times he had falls and was only saved by the net.

Otto kept him doing trickier and trickier stuff until, finally, Skeets had another fall. This time only luck saved him from breaking his neck. But instead of being glad that the kid was still alive, Otto acted as if he'd wished Skeets had killed himself. Or so it seemed to Skeets, anyway.

Then and there, Skeets decided to run away. The only people he knew to go to were Bimbo and his wife. They had retired from circus life after being fired by Otto and bought a small house. Skeets had their address, and one night he beat it. He took with him just a few clothes and the small trunk which held the stuff his parents had left him.

"I wasn't too surprised when Skeets showed up," Bimbo said. "I'd figured that life with Otto might get too unpleasant. But when Skeets told us what had happened—about his belongings being searched and about Otto making him work out on the high trapeze—I knew it was more than that. It was very clear that Skeets' life was in danger."

We had now left the woods and were crossing the field. The warm sunlight after the gloom of the woods should have felt good. But not to me. I was too chilled by Bimbo's story to notice anything. Creeps! This was no two-bit mystery. This was for real!

Brains had been listening quietly all the while, but now he spoke up.

"I take it that when Otto searched Skeets' effects, he was seeking the paper that Mr. Fenton had hidden."

"I'm sure of it," Bimbo said. "And when he couldn't find it, he put Skeets in a position where he might fall and kill himself—*accidentally*, of course."

"Would Otto then gain full control of the circus?" Brains asked.

"Undoubtedly," Bimbo said. "Skeets has no relatives. And as his partner and guardian, Otto would get everything. It would do no good to go to the police. We hadn't a nickel's worth of proof."

Skeets had caught up with Marjory and was walking beside the elephant. There was something about the slump of Skeets' shoulders and the way he stared down at the ground that let you know how he was feeling. What an awful fix he was in. No father or mother and now this goon Otto gunning for him.

"I was positive Otto would come after Skeets," Bimbo said, "and just as positive that he would head for my place first. Well, he did. We managed to get Skeets out of sight and I stalled Otto off. But I knew he'd be back."

Well, Bimbo and his wife didn't sit around making up their minds what to do. They quickly packed up and left, with Skeets of course. The move was complicated by Marjory, the elephant. She was Bimbo's own property and when he'd been fired by Otto he'd taken Marjory with him. But Bimbo put the elephant in the special covered trailer he had and they hit the road.

They drove for a couple of days, looking for some out-of-the-way place where they'd be safe from Otto. Then, as luck would have it, they passed through Crestwood and saw the Madden house and the *For Rent* sign.

"It seemed like a perfect hideout," Bimbo said. "It was far away from neighbors and the story of it being haunted would help keep people away. I certainly didn't want anybody snooping around."

He glanced over at me and something close to a smile came to his lips. He had been so tense looking that the change was startling.

"That's why I tried to scare you off when you came about the paper. The last thing we needed was a newsboy showing up every afternoon."

"But I didn't see you," I said. "I saw those two crazy guys, Montgomery and Gustav."

"You saw me," Bimbo said.

"Huh?" I let out.

Brains looked as puzzled as I felt. Then his expression changed.

"Oh," he said. "I see."

Well, I didn't. In fact it took me about a full minute more to catch on. Even then I wasn't too sure.

"You mean *you* were Montgomery and Gustav?" I gasped.

Bimbo nodded. "That's right. Being a clown I was an old hand at quick changes. I had a few of my circus outfits with me and I thought I'd give Skeets a little fun and at the same time startle you so you'd never come back."

"Whew!" I said. "You almost did."

So that was it. Montgomery and Gustav didn't even exist. What an actor Bimbo the clown was.

We had almost reached the house by this time. Skeets was already crossing the back yard, leading Marjory toward the barn. Even though everything was now a lot different, the old Madden place still gave me the creeps.

Bimbo's account had cleared up almost all of the things that had been bothering us—except for one big question. I was just about to put it to him when I stopped dead in my tracks.

At that exact moment a bloodcurdling scream came from the house. And that same terrible voice screeched,

"Cut his throat! Cut his throat!"

CHAPTER 7

Emergency

I GUESS the only reason Brains and I didn't take off for the woods the way we'd done before was because of Bimbo. He acted as if he hadn't even heard the scream.

"What . . . what was that?" I finally got out.

"What was what?" Bimbo asked.

He glanced at me, frowning a little.

"Oh, you mean the Senator," he finally said. "I completely forgot that you boys don't know him. I'm so used to the old fellow. Come inside and you can meet him. And the Queen, too."

Here we had just got off one dizzy merry-go-round, only

to be plopped right back on another. Who in the world were the Senator and the Queen?

I sneaked a look over at Brains. But he was wearing that dead-pan expression of his and I couldn't even guess what he was thinking. If Bimbo had only gone into the house ahead of us, I might have had a chance to talk to my partner. I sure wanted to. But Bimbo opened the back door and stood aside.

"Step in, boys," he said. "Skeets will be along in a moment, after he's put Marjory in the barn."

It was dark and gloomy beyond the door and I hesitated.

"After you," I said politely to Brains.

He shot me a poisonous look. Then, he took off his stalking hat and entered. I marched in right behind him.

We were in the kitchen of the old house. It was huge, with a wood stove and an ancient tin sink. Seated at a table at one side of the room by a window was a dark-haired woman. She was gazing at a row of playing cards in front of her.

"Cleo," Bimbo said. "We have guests."

The woman raised her head and smiled at us. She was about Bimbo's age and was sort of dusky, like a gypsy, and real nice looking. She wore a thin scarf-like thing on her head. The scarf was colored purple and it had what seemed to be little gold coins sewn to it. They glittered in the light.

"I know," she said in a quiet voice. "I read it in the cards."

"Boys," Bimbo said. "I want you to meet my wife, Cleopatra—otherwise known as the Queen, the fabulous and fascinating fortune-telling and mind-reading mystic, late of the Fenton Circus."

He chanted it like those talkers do outside a side show.

Bimbo had our business card in his hand. He glanced down at it and rattled off our names to the Queen.

Brains and I both said how-do-you-do at the same time. So the Queen was Bimbo's wife. But where was the Senator?

I started to look around and then I heard somebody say, "Any of you cheap skates got a cigar?"

The voice came from a corner of the kitchen. I darn nearly went right through the floor when I saw who had spoken. Perched on a wooden stand was a beady-eyed parrot.

"And that," Bimbo said with a wave of his arm, "is his honor, the Senator. So-called because he likes to talk."

The parrot blinked its sharp little eyes directly at me.

"Cut his throat!" it screeched. "Cut his throat!"

Well, after all our panic over that horrible yell, to find out that it had come from a parrot sort of took the wind out of you. It did me, anyway.

But Brains seemed fascinated by the Senator and he went closer.

"Astonishing enunciation," he said. "I never would have believed it."

"Aw, shut up," the Senator shrilled.

"Amazing," Brains said.

The parrot fluttered its wings and strutted sideways along the bar of its perch.

"Go wash your neck!" it screeched.

It was a good-sized bird, gray colored with a bright splash of red at the base of its tail. Its feet and beak were blackish.

"An excellent specimen of the African Gray," Brains said. He turned toward Bimbo. "Where did you obtain him?"

Bimbo didn't answer. He had gone over to the table and was leaning on it, talking quietly to his wife. All the good humor and gag stuff was gone now. He was deadly serious and so was the Queen.

I guess Bimbo was giving her a quick rundown of what had happened. But I couldn't hear anything that was being said until the Queen raised her voice a little bit.

"Are you sure it was the Joker?" she asked, sharply.

Bimbo leaned farther across the table, his voice still so low I couldn't catch the words. He must have convinced his wife for she picked up the cards with one sweep of her hand and pushed back her chair.

"I should have known when the jack of spades kept appearing," she said. "We'll have to leave. Right away!"

Just then, Skeets came through the open door. Gulliver, the little dog, was with him.

"I'm going," Skeets said. "By myself."

"Not alone, you aren't," Bimbo said.

"I can't have you racing all over the country just for me," Skeets said. "You've done enough."

"Now listen to me," the Queen said. "Your father and mother were the best friends Bimbo and I ever had. We're looking after you."

Bimbo punched his right fist against the palm of his left hand.

"If there was only somewhere you could hide out for a few days until we could make definite plans."

The three of them were there in a group, talking away, as if Brains and I didn't exist. I sidled toward Brains.

"We'd better beat it," I whispered.

And brother, did I want to. Playing around with a simple mystery might be fun. But getting mixed up with a guy like Otto was something else again.

"Shhhh," Brains said. "I wish to hear. I'm beginning to get an idea."

I didn't like the sound of *that*. Brains and his ideas usually spelled trouble.

Skeets was arguing with Bimbo and the Queen about what they should do. I noticed a funny sort of tremble in his voice. He was close to bawling. Jeepers, I felt sorry for him.

"Please . . . please, let me go by myself," he said. "If you go you'll have to leave Marjory. The wheel's off the trailer."

Bimbo slapped his hand hard on his bald head.

"Great guns!" he exclaimed. "I forgot about that."

He straightened up and started for the door. He'd been fairly calm up to now. But what Skeets had told him seemed to put him into a panic.

"I'll have to try to fix it right away," he said.

He stopped suddenly and turned back.

"Where's the circus playing, Cleo?"

"Middlebury," she said.

Bimbo snapped his fingers. "That's forty miles away. It'll take the Joker a while to drive back there. And there's an afternoon show. Otto will have to be on hand . . . Yes, we've got a little time. Otto isn't likely to make a move before tonight."

"Unless the Joker phones him the news," the Queen said. "And Otto comes right away."

Bimbo winced.

"Go pack your things, both of you," he said. "And hurry! I'll do my best with that wheel."

Bimbo made for the door again and then he saw us. In his agitation it was clear he had completely forgotten us.

"You boys better go home," he said. "I don't want you mixed up in this. I shouldn't have told you all the things I did. But you already knew so much . . . Thank you again for saving Skeets. And please remember, not a word of what you've heard or seen to anyone. It would just make matters worse."

He would have been out the door if Brains hadn't piped up.

"Just a minute, sir," he said. "I have a suggestion."

"What is it?" Bimbo asked. "Quick! We haven't much time."

"You remarked that you wished there were some place where Skeets would be safe from detection for a few days," Brains said.

"Yes," Bimbo said. "But just try to find such a spot."

"My partner and I know of one."

"What's that?" Bimbo demanded.

"I propose that we take Skeets there," Brains went on steadily. "Then, if and when this Otto appears, you and your wife can inform him that the boy is not here. Allow him to search the premises, if necessary."

"You know of a real hide-out?" Bimbo said. "Where Skeets can't be traced?"

Brains bowed his head. "The odds would at least be in our favor," he said.

"Where is it?" Skeets asked excitedly.

Brains moved toward the table. He motioned to Bimbo and Skeets and the Queen to come closer. Then, when they had, he lowered his voice, like a spy about to give the details of how to blow up an ammunition factory, and began to speak.

I didn't have to listen to know the horrifying truth. My partner was offering to take Skeets to town and hide him from this maniac Otto in the crime lab over the garage!

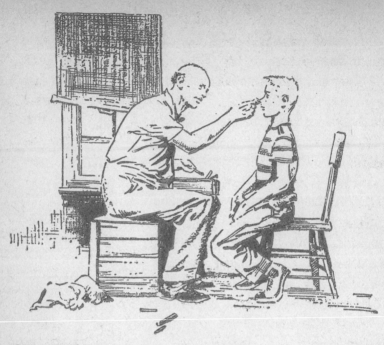

CHAPTER 8

The Plan

B Y THE time Brains was through his spiel, you could tell that Bimbo and the Queen and especially Skeets were practically sold on the idea.

"You mean even your parents wouldn't know I was hiding in the garage?" Skeets asked.

"Not if we exercise due caution," Brains said. "They have given me full possession of the rooms. No one enters without my permission. In any case, my father and mother are away most of the day. We would, however, have to smuggle you in unobserved by our housekeeper, Mrs. Ray. But that should be no problem."

Oh, yeah? I thought. This Mrs. Ray was a fussy little woman who looked after the Bentons' house and she had a pair of eyes as sharp as the Senator's. It made her mad that she'd never been allowed in the crime lab. And I'd always felt she meant to get in some day.

"How about it?" Skeets asked, turning to Bimbo and the Queen. "It sounds like the answer."

The Queen frowned. "Is there a bed in this place?" she asked.

"The crime laboratory of the Benton and Carson International Detective Agency is well equipped," Brains said loftily. "There are sleeping accommodations as well as a small bathroom."

"And food?" the Queen said. "Skeets will have to eat."

"My partner and I both live at home," Brains replied. "It should not be too difficult for us to . . . ah . . . obtain the necessary provisions."

I could almost see myself pulling stuff off the kitchen shelves without Mom knowing. Creeps! This was going to be *just* great!

Bimbo was passing his hand back and forth across his bald head. He seemed to be doing a lot of thinking. After all, here he was being talked into handing over Skeets to a couple of guys he scarcely knew. Yet, I suppose the fix they were all in was so bad that he was ready to try almost anything.

"I don't know what to say," Bimbo muttered. "You boys will be sticking your necks out. Otto is a dangerous man. If he ever learns that you've hidden Skeets, you might . . . well, you might get hurt."

I was miles ahead of him.

"I foresee little or no danger," Brains said.

Brother, the way he tossed that off, you'd think we were going on a Sunday School picnic to the park.

"Let me do it, Bimbo," Skeets said. "It's my chance to get away before Otto shows up. He'll never figure I'm with these kids."

"Well," Bimbo said. He dragged out the word. "I suppose we could try it for a day or so until I can make other arrangements."

He looked over at me and maybe he read my thoughts.

"Are you sure you are both in full agreement?" he asked.

"Indeed we are," Brains said. "Correct, Jimmy?"

"Correct," I said.

But I darn near strangled on the word.

Everything went into high gear with a bang after that. Brains worked out most of the details. I was to change clothes with Skeets. Then Skeets, disguised as me, was to strike out for the crime lab with Brains. This was so that anybody seeing the two of them would think that Skeets was me and not a stranger. Understand? Bimbo was going to use his make-up stuff on Skeets so the disguise would be even better.

As for me, I was to head for the garage by a different route, wearing Skeets' clothes, of course.

"But what if I run into my mother?" I asked. "She'll be sure to notice I haven't got on my own stuff. And she'll ask why."

"Then don't run into her," Brains said. He pulled at his long nose thoughtfully. "We'd better take all of Skeets' possessions with us. Nothing of his should be left here for Otto to find."

"Good idea," Bimbo said. You could see he was sort of impressed by Brains. "Skeets hasn't much. Just one bag and that small trunk of his parents."

"Come along, child," the Queen said to Skeets. "I'll help you pack. Quickly now."

While they were gone, Brains and I took off our stalking suits and Brains put them into his kit bag. We had just washed the burnt cork off our faces when Skeets and the Queen came hurrying back, carrying a zippered bag and the trunk. The trunk was small, all right, about the size of a double suitcase. It was old-timey looking with a big brass handle to carry it by and metal corner pieces.

Right away, without losing any time, Skeets and I went into a side room and changed clothes. He was about my size and his pants and checkered sport shirt fitted me fine. He looked O.K. in my jeans and striped T-shirt, too.

Bimbo had us sit down side by side in the kitchen and he got busy with his make-up kit. He colored Skeets' hair and eyebrows brown with a powder, and painted freckles like mine on his face. He even used actor's putty to change the shape of Skeets' nose.

When he was through I guess my father and mother would've known that Skeets wasn't me. But from a distance, we did look pretty much alike. Brains thought so, anyway.

Things had been really humming with everybody racing around and the Queen keeping watch at the windows for any sign of the Joker coming back. I guess all the excitement got the parrot stirred up.

"Cut his throat! Cut his throat!" he screeched.

Then, "Aw, shut up . . . Go wash your neck."

Every once in a while he let go with an imitation of Skeets' whistle. It was driving the little dog crazy. Gulliver kept racing around and barking as he tried to find out who had called him.

The noise got so bad that the Queen finally said, "Hush the Senator, Skeets. For goodness' sake."

The parrot bobbed along its perch and eyed her.

"Hello, madam," he squawked at the Queen. "You look like an unmade bed."

Even though I was all tensed up, I couldn't help but laugh. And when I did, the Senator went, "Ha! Ha!" too.

Skeets got a package of seeds and dumped them into the parrot's cup.

"That'll pipe him down," Skeets said. "He's crazy about sunflower seeds."

The Senator was going for them. I could see that.

"I guess you know I'll have to take the Senator with me," Skeets said to Brains.

"Take him with you!" Brains exclaimed. "Why?"

"He won't eat for anybody else," Skeets said.

"That's right," Bimbo said. "The bird is Skeets' special pet. He brought him along when he ran away from the circus. He'd die without Skeets."

"Good gravy!" I said. "Somebody's sure to hear him in the crime lab. We'll be in real trouble if he starts yelling that throat-cutting stuff."

Boy, I could just imagine what Mrs. Ray, the Bentons' housekeeper, would do. She'd call the cops but fast. And she'd be right behind them when they broke into the lab.

Brains was gnawing at his lip. This was something he sure hadn't thought of.

"If we must take him, we must," he said. "I'll construct a soundproof box for him."

"Aw, shut up!" the Senator shrieked.

"Until you do, I can keep him pretty quiet with sunflower seeds," Skeets said. "But how are we going to carry him? We'll be loaded down with my trunk and bag and the things you have."

"The solution is quite simple," Brains said. "My partner will bring him."

"Me?" I said.

"Certainly. You will be empty-handed. We'll place the Senator in a cardboard box and wrap it up like an ordinary package—with holes punched in the sides for air."

"Go wash your neck!" the parrot shrilled.

I didn't like the idea one little bit. What if the fool bird began sounding off as I went through town?

"Put plenty of those seeds in," I told Skeets.

Well, Bimbo found a big box and Skeets finally got the Senator into it—but not without a struggle. The parrot fought hard, beating its wings and trying to peck Skeets' hand.

"Help! Help!" the Senator kept screaming. "I'm drowning! Drowning."

Just before the top was closed, Skeet dumped in a handful of seeds. They seemed to quiet down the parrot but I could hear him sort of squawking to himself as Bimbo wrapped brown paper around the box.

At last everything seemed set for our take-off. It was way past noon by this time and I was worried about what my mother was going to say. She expected me home for lunch.

"I wish there were some way we could keep in touch with you," Bimbo said. "Unfortunately, we have no telephone."

"I'll be frantic until I hear that Skeets has arrived safely," the Queen said.

Brains had to think a moment before he came up with the answer. But it didn't take him long.

"Very well," he said. "We will set up communication lines this way. Every afternoon, my partner here will deliver a copy of the *Crestwood Daily Ledger* to the house. Inside the paper I will write a cryptic report of how we are faring. If anybody should be spying on the house, it will appear to be just a routine delivery of the evening newspaper."

"Say," Bimbo exclaimed. "That's smart."

Brains tried to shrug off the praise.

"Elementary," he said in his best Sherlock Holmes manner.

It *was* smart, except for one thing. The guy who had to pull it off was nobody but little old Operative Three.

"Now if you should wish to send us a message and you suspect that the house is being watched," Brains went on, "conceal your communication under the mat outside the front door. My partner will then pick it up when he deposits the paper."

"Good," Bimbo said. He grinned at me. "You wanted me to take a subscription to your paper. Now you can sign me up."

I just happened to have a pad of blank forms on me, so

I had Bimbo fill out one. I was a little surprised when he wrote down his name as *Leopold Duval*. Somehow it didn't fit him. But Bimbo did.

Well, I thought, when he dug into his pocket and paid me for a year's subscription, I'd made a sale after all.

While this was going on, Brains and Skeets were loading themselves up with the trunk and bag and Brains' equipment. After we'd all carefully looked through the window for any sign of spies lurking in the field, Brains and Skeets slipped out the back door.

Bimbo and the Queen and I watched them plough through the tall grass as they headed for the woods. Bimbo held the dog, Gulliver, in his arms.

"The last thing I want Gulliver to do is go after Skeets," Bimbo said. "And he might easily."

"Oh, dear," the Queen said, "I do hope everything works out. But I'm so nervous. That Otto is such an awful creature."

Bimbo and I stayed at the window until Brains and Skeets had disappeared into the woods. I noticed that the Queen had gone back to the table and was putting down a row of playing cards. She sure looked like a fortuneteller as she studied them.

"The future is murky," I heard her say half to herself, "and black with trouble. And forces of evil loom large."

A few minutes later I left the Madden house by the front door, carrying the Senator in the wrapped box. And as I walked down the lane to the road, I seemed to hear the Queen's voice saying those words over and over again.

It was a hot day—but I shivered.

CHAPTER 9

Perilous Journey

Nobody much ever used the narrow dusty road that swung past the Madden place. Even so, I felt I was lucky to reach the edge of town without meeting anyone. The Senator had kept quiet except for one outburst and that had been my fault. I'd tripped over a rock and jolted the box and he'd let go a shriek that could've been heard in the next county.

"Cut his throat! Cut his throat!"

You can bet I was extra careful how I carried the box when I started through Crestwood. I didn't take the shortest route to the garage even though I was in a dither to find out if Skeets and Brains had arrived safely. Instead, I went in a roundabout way by Vine Street and Balsam. This was so I'd steer clear of my house and avoid the chance of meeting my mother.

I should have had my head read.

I was halfway down Balsam and passing the house where the principal of my school lived when the front door opened and old Horsey, himself, came out. Everybody at school called Mr. Peters Horsey because . . . well, he looked like a horse.

Horsey had a man and woman with him.

"Why hello, James," Horsey called out to me.

I started to walk faster. I could hear the Senator stirring around inside the box and making a sort of clucking noise.

"Just a minute, my boy," Horsey said. "I want you to meet someone."

I stopped. What else could I do?

Horsey and the man and woman ambled out to the side-walk where I was.

"This is Mr. Cummings, James," Horsey said. "He's taking Miss O'Donnell's place and will be in charge of your group at school. You are the first pupil he's met."

Creeps! The new teacher.

"How do you do, Jimmy," Mr. Cummings said.

Then I was introduced to his wife. She was small and pretty-pretty and had on a lot of lipstick goo. The way she hung to her husband's arm you'd think she was scared he was going to get away.

"Ohhhh, what a *big* package for such a *little* boy," she said.

She was *that* kind.

She reached out to touch the box and I almost had heart failure.

"What's in it?" she sort of cooed. "Or is it a *secret?*"

I moved the box out of her reach.

"A flying machine," I said.

It was the first thing I could think of. And after all it was no lie.

"Oh, my," she said. "How *interesting*."

I could feel the Senator moving around more and more. I knew that unless I got away fast something might happen.

"I'd . . . I'd better go," I said. "I'm late for lunch."

"Well, it's been nice seeing you, Jimmy," Mr. Cummings said. "Goodbye now."

"Goodbye, sir," I said.

And away I went. From behind me I heard Mrs. Cummings say,

"How sweet."

"You'll find we have exceptionally nice children here in Crestwood," Horsey said. "Well mannered . . . no bad habits . . ."

At that moment I stumbled over a raised part of the sidewalk. To my horror I heard the Senator yell,

"Any of you cheap skates got a cigar?"

I don't know what Horsey or Mr. and Mrs. Cummings thought or said. I didn't hang around to find out. I just plain ran. And I didn't slow down until I reached the street where Brains lived.

"You dope," I said to the Senator. "Keep that big trap of yours shut, will you!"

Brains and I had decided that he and Skeets would slip into the garage by the secret door while I'd come openly down the driveway past his house and go in the regular way. Well, I was almost at the entrance to the driveway and was thinking that at last I was safe, when I heard somebody call,

"Jimmy!"

I looked up, startled. It was that drip, Stony Rhodes. He was riding along the street toward me.

"Hi," I said as casually as I could.

At any other time I would've told him about signing up a new subscriber. But not now.

"How'd you get over here?" he asked.

He was gazing at me as if I had two heads or something. "I just saw you a minute ago on Oak Street with Brains," he went on.

That jolted me. He'd seen Skeets disguised as me, of course.

"I get around," I said. "I'm a fast worker."

I kept right on moving along until I hit the drive and turned into it.

"But it's impossible," Stony called after me. "You couldn't have got here that fast."

"It's done with mirrors," I yelled back.

Let him chew on that for a while, I thought.

I fully expected Mrs. Ray, the Benton's housekeeper, to pop out on the back porch before I could get to the garage at the end of the drive. She had a habit of trying to stick her nose into our business. Thank goodness, she didn't appear.

But, brother, I sure let go a gasp of relief when I was in the main part of the garage, where Mr. Benton kept his car. The regular stairs that led to the rooms above were at the back. I went up them two at a time and gave the code knock.

Brains opened the door. Skeets was right behind him. Was I ever glad to see those two.

They'd just arrived a minute or so before. Everything had gone fine, Brains told me.

"We didn't encounter anyone I knew except that friend of yours, Stony Rhodes," Brains said. "And he was across the street."

"Yeah," I said. "I ran into him, too. He's probably still trying to figure out the double exposure . . . And listen, he's no friend of mine."

Skeets was looking around the lab. You could see he was amazed at everything. But I didn't let him do much sightseeing. I shoved the box at him.

"Get the Senator out," I said, "and give him some seeds before he starts yelling."

Skeets unfastened the cord around the box and I helped him pull off the wrapping paper. We could hear the parrot fluttering and stewing inside.

Just then, a buzzer on Brains' desk sounded. It was the signal that somebody was calling from the Benton house. Brains had put up his own private telephone from the house to the lab.

"That will be Mrs. Ray," Brains groaned.

He clicked on a switch and spoke into a small microphone.

"Barclay!" The voice came from a wall speaker. "I've been trying and trying and trying to reach you. Where on earth have you been?"

It was Mrs. Ray, all right. You couldn't mistake her voice.

"Out for a stroll with Jimmy," Brains replied.

"Well!" Mrs. Ray said. "James' mother has telephoned. He is wanted at home—immediately. And I've had your lunch on the table for at least forty-five minutes."

By this time, Skeets had the top of the box open and the Senator came bursting out. His feathers were all messed up and he was mad as hops.

Mrs. Ray's voice was going on. "It's absurd the way your parents let you practically live in that awful place. Some day they'll be sorry. No good will come of it."

"Aw, shut up!" the Senator screeched.

My heart almost stopped. Mrs. Ray was sure to have heard. I grabbed up Brains' jacket and threw it over the parrot. We were in trouble up to our ears now.

But, once again, I didn't figure on Brains' fast thinking. He brought the mike to his lips and spoke into it.

"Mrs. Ray! What was that you said?" He sounded shocked.

"What did *I* say?" The housekeeper's voice was so shrill the speaker vibrated.

"I distinctly heard somebody say shut up," Brains said.

The woman's gulp for breath was plainly audible.

"I heard it, too. I thought *you* said it."

"Now, Mrs. Ray," Brains said. "You know I'd never use an expression like that to you. I wouldn't dream of it."

"I just can't understand it," she said. "I just can't."

"I have a possible explanation," Brains went on. "The toggle gear may have become detached from the microwave spectra, thus affecting the efficiency of the differential magnetic variometer. If that is so, then it is possible that we are picking up camshaft vibrations from some broadcasting station."

"I see," Mrs. Ray said.

"I must try to locate the trouble," Brains said. "In the meantime, I will convey to Jimmy the information that he is to report to his home. Also, I shall be in for lunch, directly. Thank you, Mrs. Ray. You've been splendidly cooperative. Goodbye."

Brains clicked off. By this time I was practically rolling on the floor, laughing. Skeets, of course, had caught on to the double talk. He was grinning, too, as he fed the Senator a heap of sunflower seeds.

"She will worry over that for a week, poor creature," Brains said. "Come on, Jimmy. We had better depart."

Brains turned to Skeets. "Sorry that we have to leave you alone. However, we shall be back very shortly. And with some food. In the meantime, make yourself comfortable. I intend to construct soundproof quarters for the bird when I return."

"Try to keep him quiet," I said.

"I'll make out," Skeets said. "See you."

At the door, Brains grabbed me by the arm.

"Wait a minute," he said. "You can't go out like that."

"Why not?" I asked. "What's wrong?"

"You are still wearing Skeets' clothes," he said.

Creeps!

Well, it didn't take long to change outfits with Skeets, and then Brains and I beat it.

"Try not to be long in returning, Operative Three," Brains said when he reached the back door of his house. "This afternoon I am determined to thoroughly examine that trunk of Skeets' and everything his parents left him for some sign of that missing paper."

"I'll be back in a flash," I said.

I'll admit I hadn't been too eager about getting mixed up in this case. Yet now that we were in it, I was pretty excited. And I sure wanted to be on hand when that trunk was opened.

But when I got home, I was in for a big surprise. For one thing, our car was parked beside the house and it had been freshly washed and polished. For another, my dad was in the kitchen with Mom. He usually stayed downtown for lunch.

"You're terribly late, Jimmy," Mom said. "Honestly, I don't know what I'm going to do with you. Now eat your lunch and go up and wash and put on your good clothes. I've laid them out on your bed."

"What's the big idea?" I asked. "I'm not going anywhere."

My dad had his hands in his side pockets and he was rocking back and forth on his heels and smiling.

"Yes, you are, son," he said. "I was able to get some time off from the office this week and guess what?"

"What?" I said.

"We're all driving up to Ann's camp," my dad said. "And we're going to stay over and visit her for a couple of days."

CHAPTER 10

Dangerous Mission

OH, NO!" I said.

I couldn't leave town now and miss everything.

"What's wrong with you?" my father asked.

"I . . . I can't go," I said. "I just can't!"

My mother was putting away some stuff in the dining room and the swinging door had closed.

"What's this?" she called.

"Jimmy claims he can't go with us," Dad said.

"For goodness' sake," Mom said. She came hustling back into the kitchen. "Why not?"

"I've got things to do," I said.

"Oh, that's ridiculous," Mom said. "Eat your lunch and get ready. Don't you want to see your sister?"

"No," I said.

Ann was O.K. but right now all I wanted to see was what was in that trunk.

"James MacDonald Carson," Mom said. "You should be ashamed of yourself. Here your father and I have planned a nice surprise and you act this way."

"Creeps, Mom," I said. "I can't help it. Brains and I are working on something. If I go away now it'll ruin everything."

My dad was standing there, looking at me. He was a big man with muscles. He'd been a fullback in college and he could still handle a football. He'd taught me a lot about sports. It was easy to learn from him. He seemed to understand kids.

"If the boy doesn't want to go, there's no sense making his life miserable, Clara," he said to my mother.

"We can't leave him here by himself," Mom said.

"I could stay with Brains," I said. "There's an extra bed in his room."

Hey! That would be perfect. No more dashing back and forth from my house to his. I'd be on the home grounds.

"It might not suit the Bentons right now," my mother said.

"Sure it will," I said.

I could sense that Mom was weakening. She was really a softy even though she sometimes acted tough.

"Remember what Mrs. Benton said after Brains stayed here, Mom?" I went on. "That time they had to go to a wedding or a funeral or something? 'We'd just love to have Jimmy *anytime*,' she said. Remember that, Mom?"

"Yes," Mom said. "But . . ."

"I'll phone them and find out if it's O.K.," I cut in quickly.

I dashed to the telephone in the downstairs hall before anybody could say anything more and I dialed the Bentons' number. For once Mrs. Ray didn't answer. Brains did.

I gave him the score fast and he caught on right away.

"Certainly you may visit here," he said. "But just for the record, let me verify it with my mother. She has just come in."

Well, Mrs. Benton got on the phone and Mom took over from me and there was a lot of palaver. But finally, everything was set. I was to park at Brains'.

It didn't take me long to gobble down my lunch and throw pajamas and stuff into a suitcase. Then, I said goodbye to Mom and Dad and sent my best to my dear sister Ann, and I took off. But just before I left, I had a chance to shove two cans of beans, a stick of butter, three eggs and half a loaf of bread in my bag for Skeets.

Brains was already in the lab when I arrived. He was busily nailing sections of wallboard together to make what he called an "isolation booth" for the Senator. Brains had smuggled in some food, too, as well as an electric burner. And Skeets was having himself a meal.

The Senator hadn't made a sound while we'd been gone, Skeets reported. The parrot was now perched on the back of a chair, gnawing on a piece of lettuce Brains had brought him. He looked plain sleepy to me. And I guess he was after that small mountain of sunflower seeds we'd fed him.

Brains got the isolation booth finished and the Senator let Skeets move him to a perch inside his new home without any fuss.

"Now," Brains said to Skeets. "With your permission my partner and I would like to examine your trunk and its contents."

"Help yourself," Skeets said. "But I don't think you'll have any luck finding the missing paper. Bimbo and I have gone over everything a dozen times. We even searched the lining and poked around for a false bottom."

"We would still appreciate the opportunity to make a thorough investigation," Brains said.

"Go ahead," Skeets said. "I sure hope you find it. It's the only thing that'll stop Otto, seems like."

The scared expression had been gone from Skeets' face. But now it was back.

"I wonder how Bimbo and the Queen are doing?" he said abruptly. "Maybe Otto's come already."

"Bimbo figured he wouldn't do anything before tonight at the earliest," I said.

"I know . . . I know," Skeets said. "But you can't tell. Otto's a pretty slick guy. He pulls things you don't expect."

Brains had moved the small trunk across the room and I helped him lift it up on a work bench. The trunk was made of hard wood and from the scratches and gouges, it had done a lot of traveling. I hadn't looked it over closely before and for the first time I noticed the tricky design of the brass handle you carried it by. There was a bulge of metal at the top of the handle that had been neatly molded into the form of a clown's head.

Skeets saw me examining it.

"That's the trademark of my father's circus," he said. "He had the clown's head put on just about everything . . . Do you know who was the model for that head?"

"Bimbo?" Brains said.

"Right. Bimbo sat for the sculptor who did the job. And it's just the way he used to look in his clown's costume."

The clown on the brass handle was grinning broadly. He had a ball of a nose, big pointed ears that jutted out, and diamond-shaped eyes. Maybe it was because Skeets had told us, but now I could see that it did look like Bimbo.

The lock of the trunk hadn't worked for years, according to Skeets, and the lid was held down by two clamps. Brains flipped the clamps up.

He glanced at me, just before he opened the lid.

"Ready?" he asked.

He was as excited as I was—if that was possible.

"Shoot," I said.

I don't know exactly what I expected to see in the trunk. But when the lid was thrown back and I stared inside, I was disappointed. There seemed to be nothing but odds and ends of costumes and bits of circus equipment.

Half an hour later, after everything had been dumped out and given a quick once-over, I was still disappointed. We'd found plenty of other things in the trunk besides costumes. A stack of old circus programs tied together. A scrapbook of newspaper clippings about Skeets' parents. A folded poster advertising the first opening of the Fenton Circus years ago. A couple of photo albums jammed with pictures of Mr. and Mrs. Fenton back in Hull, England, before they left for the U.S., and any number of circus shots showing them flipping from one trapeze to another and posing with other performers. There was a whole section of pictures of Skeets, too, making his first try at walking a wire, hanging from a low trapeze and riding on top of Marjory, the elephant, with Bimbo.

We unearthed three boxes jammed with jewelry, a walking cane with a gold top and a whole heap more.

I knew what Skeets had meant when he'd said his father had put the clown's head on just about everything. He sure had. It was on the top of the boxes, and on a silver cigarette case. It had even been used, in small size, on stick pins and cuff links. And the gold knob of the walking stick was in the form of Bimbo's head, too.

There was plenty of stuff to look at, all right. But, for my money, there wasn't even the smell of a secret paper anywhere.

Brains wasn't satisfied by one run-through. He started back, examining every item carefully before putting it aside. He tapped the gold head of the cane to make sure it wasn't hollow. And he took a long time over each metal box.

While this was going on, Skeets was wandering around the lab. He couldn't keep still. Every so often he'd say,

"Find anything?"

And when Brains would shake his head, Skeets would start pacing again.

"I shouldn't have run off from Bimbo and the Queen," he said once. "Otto might do something terrible to them to try to make them tell where I am."

"Stop worrying," Brains said. "I feel certain that Bimbo and his wife can take care of themselves."

"Maybe you're right," Skeets said. "But you don't know Otto."

I hadn't paid any attention to the clock until Brains suddenly said,

"It's after four, Jimmy."

Creeps! I had to get down to the *Ledger* office and pick up my papers.

"I am sure you have not forgotten about the new subscriber on your list," Brains said. "And that you are to act as secret courier between us and Bimbo."

"How could I forget?" I said.

The idea of going back to the Madden house alone had been in the back of my mind for hours. Not that the old house scared me any more. But the chance of maybe running into Otto and the Joker did.

"Say," Skeets exclaimed. "That's right. What message will we send Bimbo and the Queen?"

"I have already composed the dispatch," Brains said. "I have made it cryptic intentionally in the event the courier should fall into enemy hands."

My partner could say the most comforting things.

"Operative Three," Brains said, now very much the master sleuth, "you will write these words at the top of the second page of the paper to be deposited on the doorstep of the Madden house. Memorize them well."

"I will when you tell me what they are," I said.

He paid no attention to me.

"Here is the message: CARGO ARRIVED. NO BREAKAGE."

"Cargo arrived. No breakage," I repeated. "Got it!"

"I believe that will convey the fact that Skeets is here and that all is well. One thing more, Operative Three. Be sure you look under the door mat for any message to be brought back. And report here as soon as possible. Good luck!"

I felt like saluting.

I went home and got my bike and the delivery bag with *Crestwood Daily Ledger* lettered across it before heading downtown. At the newspaper office I gave Mr. Worts, the circulation manager, the order form Bimbo had filled out and he said that I was doing great in the contest but that Stony Rhodes was still ahead of me. Somehow I didn't much care at the moment.

All in all, I was late picking up my bundle of papers and the other kids had gone.

The Madden house was the farthest away of all my customers and the last on my list. It was almost six o'clock when I started out the dirt road to deliver Bimbo's paper. I had already written CARGO ARRIVED. NO BREAKAGE across the top of the second page, just the way Brains had wanted.

The road was again deserted. I didn't see a soul, not even a rabbit. And everything was so still as I rode up the lane to the old house that it didn't seem natural.

When I put down my bike and went to the front door, I heard the little dog, Gulliver, barking inside. And I found myself wondering if Bimbo and the Queen were there, too. Or had something happened to them?

I placed the newspaper carefully on the doormat. At the same time I lifted a corner of the mat with my other hand.

A piece of paper was there, neatly folded.

I had the horrible feeling that I was being watched and I quickly closed my hand over the piece of paper, crumpling it. At that moment, I heard a sharp tapping sound from one of the windows. It might as well have been a bomb exploding from the way I jumped.

I raised my head. It was Bimbo. He winked at me and smiled and held up his hand, making a circle with his thumb and first finger. He was signaling that everything was O.K.

I sure was relieved. Even so I was in a hurry to get away. Somebody might be watching the house.

I didn't read Bimbo's note until I was back on the road to town. It just said, NO VISITORS. ALL IS WELL.

So far so good. Otto hadn't shown up yet and maybe he wouldn't. Maybe this whole thing had been a false alarm.

I had just shoved the note into my pocket when I noticed a car coming toward me from the direction of Crestwood. It was a nifty high-powered foreign convertible. The top was down and I could see two men in it.

I steered to the side of the road to give the car plenty of room to pass. But just before the convertible reached me it slowed down and I couldn't help noticing that the two men were giving me the once-over.

The driver was a beefy-faced man wearing a yellow sport coat and a white cap. I'd never seen him before. The guy beside him was thinnish and mean looking. But what startled me was what he had on—a black jacket and a black snap-brimmed hat.

It was just like the hat the Joker had worn.

The convertible rolled on past and picked up speed. Ah, forget it, I told myself. There were thousands of guys with black hats. That wasn't the Joker. And that wasn't Otto with him. They'd speed right by the Madden house without even looking at it.

To convince myself that I was right, I looked back over my shoulder. I was just in time to see the convertible pull almost to a stop. Then it turned into the lane that led to the old Madden house on the hill.

CHAPTER 11

Sudden Alarm

THE Joker and Otto *were* in that car. I was sure now. Terribly sure. Otto had come after Skeets, just as Bimbo had said he would.

I was in a ring-tailed panic. Yet I knew the only thing for me to do was to get away, and fast. If I stuck around and tried to find out what was happening, Otto or the Joker might see me and somehow manage to get a line on where Skeets was.

So I made for the lab.

Skeets almost passed out when I burst in with the news. And I'd never seen Brains so upset either.

"Otto will be wild when he doesn't find me," Skeets said. He was practically wringing his hands. "He'll try to force Bimbo and the Queen to talk."

"Now take it easy . . . take it easy," Brains said. "We must all be calm."

He was striding up and down the lab, about as relaxed as a rabbit caught in the middle of a rifle range.

"It's awful sitting here and doing nothing," Skeets said. "I almost feel like going out there."

"Are you crazy?" Brains exploded. "That'd wreck the whole scheme. We were certain this would happen. That's why you're here."

"I know . . . I know," Skeets said. "But I brought this on them. I've put them in danger . . ."

At that moment Brains' mother telephoned from the house that dinner was ready and for us to come *right away*. And she didn't mean in five minutes, either. That was because of Mr. Benton. Brains' father was easygoing and not very strict—except for one thing. He couldn't stand anybody being late for meals.

It was tough having to leave Skeets all by himself, especially when he was so worked up. But Brains and I cleared out of the lab on the double. We sure didn't want to have to answer a lot of questions about why we were late.

Before we took off, we had sense enough to pull the curtains across all the windows. It would be a fine thing if somebody caught sight of Skeets in there.

We had a bang-up dinner—roast beef, pan-browned potatoes, green peas and salad. And for dessert we had apple pie and ice cream. I'll say this for Mrs. Ray. Even though she was a pain in the neck she sure could bake pies.

I ate a lot. So did Brains. But it wasn't much fun stuffing yourself and thinking about Skeets making a meal out of a can of beans and bread and butter. And on top of that, I was worried about him. I mean that he might do something haywire, he'd been in such a dither over Bimbo and the Queen.

I was hoping dinner would be over in a hurry so we could get back to the lab. And it would have been except for Brains' father.

Mr. Benton was a professor of ancient history. He was a tall lanky man, a lot older than my dad and different too. He'd rather read a book than go to a football game. See?

Well, Mr. Benton was writing a paper or something on the Punic Wars. I think that was what it was. And he got on a real talking jag. He gave us a play-by-play account of how a bunch of old characters battled it out in Italy or some place. I guess it might have been interesting if you hadn't anything else on your mind. Brains' mother and Mrs. Ray thought so. But Mr. Benton lost me after the second battle.

Do you know what time it was before Mr. Benton reached the part where the Romans and the guys they were fighting decided to call it quits? Eight-thirty! And I think Mr. Benton might have kept on going if he hadn't been wanted on the telephone.

Brains gave me the high sign and we excused ourselves. Brains told his mother that he guessed we'd go out to the garage for a while.

"All right," she said. "But don't stay too late. You both looked tired."

As we started for the back door, Brains said to me, "I'll meet you outside. I want a drink of water."

Then he added in an undertone, so Mrs. Ray and his mother wouldn't hear, "Stand under the kitchen window."

He didn't have to whisper. Mrs. Ray had teed off on her favorite subject and was yammering away to Brains' mother about how unwise it was for us to be out in that "awful place" so much. Mrs. Benton was listening and nodding her head as if she agreed with everything that was being pitched at her, which I knew she didn't. Brains' mother was on our side. She thought that kids should have a certain amount of freedom and privacy. I'd heard her say so.

I went out and stood under the kitchen window as Brains had said. But I couldn't figure what he was up to until he leaned out and handed me what was left of the second apple pie that had been served, and the last of the ice cream.

"Take it, quick!" he hissed.

I did.

For all my worrying, Skeets was still in the lab and did he ever tie into the pie and ice cream. Even the Senator seemed to enjoy the piece of apple Skeets gave him.

"Any of you cheap skates got a cigar?" he squawked in between nibbles.

The soundproofing of the booth was working pretty well.

Well, Brains went right back to his job of hunting for the missing paper. He was pretty sure now that it wasn't in the stuff that had been in the trunk. So he began on the trunk itself, tapping the wood and listening for any hollow sound.

I jabbered away to Skeets to try to get his mind off his troubles. And before we knew it, Mrs. Ray was phoning that Brains' mother said it was time for us to come in and go to bed.

"We shall be there directly, Mrs. Ray," Brains said sweetly into the microphone.

The housekeeper's voice kept on coming from the wall speaker.

"Barclay," she said. "Did either of you boys eat up the rest of the pie and the ice cream?"

"Of course we didn't eat it," Brains said. "After that big dinner, how could we?"

"Well," Mrs. Ray said, "the pie and ice cream are gone ... It must have been one of those sneak thieves the paper has been talking about. The mayor should do something. This is an outrage."

"Some hungry person probably got it," Brains said, with a wink at Skeets. "We must think of that."

He signed off.

"I am sorry we have to leave you alone here tonight, Skeets," Brains said. "But I hope your bed will be comfortable."

"What bed?" he asked.

Brains reached out and turned what seemed to be an ordinary ink bottle on his desk.

"Why, there," he said.

You should have seen Skeets' face when a section of wall revolved and a bunk appeared. It was one of the first devices Brains had built into the lab and it sure worked slick.

"Say!" Skeets exclaimed. "That's neat!"

He went over and stretched out on the bunk.

"And it feels good, too. I'm tired."

"Well, get a good night's sleep," Brains said. "You will be perfectly safe here."

He bent down and clicked on a couple of switches that were mounted on a panel at the side of his desk.

"I have now set the burglar alarm system," Brains went on. "It is operated by photoelectric cells. If anybody should try to enter the garage during the night, a buzzer will sound and this desk light will blink. Understand?"

"Yes," Skeets said, uneasily. "But do you really think Otto might find out where I am and come here *tonight?*"

"You never can tell," Brains said. "The Benton and Carson International Detective Agency stands prepared for all emergencies. Now, if the alarm should go off, stay right here in the laboratory. Leave everything to my partner and to me. I have installed a duplicate warning system in my bedroom. It will sound at the same moment this one does. We will be alerted instantly and come to your rescue."

I didn't go for that "we" stuff, I can tell you.

After warning Skeets not to put on any lights, Brains and I left.

Brains' bedroom was on the second floor at the rear of the house. From his window you could look right across the garden at the garage. Soon as we got in the room, Brains switched on the burglar alarm there. He had built it into his radio so neatly that nobody would ever suspect. The radio stood on the night table next to Brains' bed.

"Tomorrow will tell the story of what has happened at

the Madden house," Brains said as he climbed into bed. "I hope when you go out there with the newspaper, Operative Three, you won't find any bodies."

Then he turned out the light.

Creeps! What a thought to put in a guy's mind the last thing at night.

And to make it worse Brains went to sleep right away. But I sure didn't. I lay there, my imagination whipping up a dandy set of horror pictures. And when I did drift off, I kept coming to with a start, thinking the alarm had sounded and that Otto and the Joker were breaking into the lab.

The next morning I felt awful. But when Brains and I got to the lab after breakfast, Skeets looked worse. His eyes were bloodshot and he had a hard time choking down any food.

I never put in such a day. It was plain gruesome. I tried playing cards with Skeets so he'd forget the spot he was in. But he wasn't interested. He just sat on his bunk, staring at the floor. Finally, I got him talking about his life in the circus and that seemed to help him some.

But it didn't help me. All I could think of was what I was going to find when I delivered the newspaper to the Madden house that afternoon.

Brains was lucky. He lost himself in work. With Skeets' permission he drilled small holes in the corners of the trunk on the chance that he might find a hidden compartment. He even took off the brass handle and carefully sunk a fine drill into the back of the clown's head. But it turned out to be solid metal.

I would have liked to have given Brains a hand. I can

drive a nail fairly straight and saw a board. But, I'm no mechanical wizard like Brains. So I always leave that department to him.

Brains' parents had taken off for the college as usual and after putting out our lunch, Mrs. Ray went to the beauty parlor to get her hair done. That gave us a chance to load up with food for Skeets—and for the Senator too. The parrot really went for the grapes and the banana we brought him. But Skeets didn't eat much.

We let the Senator out of his isolation booth to wander around and get a little exercise. It seemed safe enough with everybody in the house away even if he did sound off.

And the Senator did.

He told Brains to, "Shut up!"

And informed me that I should wash my neck.

I think the old guy felt better by the time we returned him to the booth.

The morning had dragged by, but the afternoon galloped. And suddenly, or so it seemed to me, it was after five and I was heading for the Madden place on my bike again.

I could feel my legs trembling as I rode up that long lane. Everything was still, as it had been the afternoon before. Only this time it seemed a dead stillness.

Brains had decided that the message to send Bimbo was, TEMPERATURE NORMAL. PATIENT FINE. And I'd written it at the top of the second sheet of the *Ledger*.

Well, I got off my bike and forced myself to approach the front door. It struck me as funny that I didn't hear Gulliver bark. Then, suddenly, the little dog came racing around the side of the house, tail wagging.

Almost immediately a voice called, "Gulliver! Come here!"

It was Bimbo.

In a moment, he rounded the corner of the house. He didn't look like himself. There was a piece of tape across his forehead and one eye was swollen as if he'd been hit there.

Instead of speaking, he merely nodded curtly to me. Then, he called Gulliver again. And when the dog went to him, Bimbo picked up the animal and walked away out of sight.

Creeps! Maybe Otto was inside the house. Maybe the Joker was, too. That might explain why Bimbo had acted like that.

I placed the *Ledger* on the doormat and sneaked a look under the corner. Just as before, a note was there. I closed my fingers over it and started back for my bike. It was then that I noticed the curtains at one of the windows move. And I caught a glimpse of somebody back of them.

It was the Queen.

She sort of passed by and then was gone. But at least I knew she was still up and around.

I didn't dare even glance at the note until I was out of sight of the Madden house. Bimbo had written:

VISITORS ARRIVED. PLAYED QUIZ GAME WITH
US BUT WE COULDN'T GIVE THE ANSWERS.
VISITORS LEFT, DISAPPOINTED, BUT STILL
INTERESTED IN THE HOUSE.

Brains and Skeets were waiting for me at the door. I gave them a quick rundown of what had happened and showed them the note.

"It is all quite clear," Brains said, after he'd read it. "The reference to the quiz game means that Otto and the Joker questioned Bimbo and the Queen about Skeets' whereabouts. And that bit about the visitors being still interested in the house—I would judge that Bimbo is informing us that he suspects that the place is watched."

I nodded. That made sense.

"At least Bimbo and the Queen are alive," Skeets said. "Did he look really banged up?"

"Well," I said. "He'd been worked over. That's for sure. But I don't think he was hurt badly. I couldn't see the Queen well enough to tell if anything had happened to her."

Skeets was far from happy.

"What can we do now?" he asked. "Just sit here and wait?"

Brains nodded. "There is no other course of action at the moment."

"But Otto and the Joker are sure to come back and question Bimbo and the Queen again," Skeets said. "And this time they might treat them even worse."

"Very true," Brains said. "That is why it is doubly important for us to find the paper your father hid."

He frowned and pulled at his nose.

"I am almost positive it isn't secreted in the trunk. Yet where else would he have put it?"

Brains walked slowly to his desk and sat down. He stayed there, scowling and sort of muttering to himself until we were called to dinner.

We had another good meal. But this time Mr. Benton

scarcely said a word. He hadn't a chance. Brains' mother and Mrs. Ray yakked the entire time about clothes and whether Mrs. Ray should wear her yellow something-or-other of her blue whatever-it-was when she went to visit her sister the next day. I couldn't see what difference it made but it sure was important to them.

Anyway, Brains and I got back to the lab early. Not that we had anything to do. That was the trouble. Skeets had had plenty to eat but he seemed sunk in gloom. And Brains just sat and read a book, *Solutions of Puzzling Crime Cases.*

I wound up playing solitaire. And I was plenty glad when it was time for us to turn in.

I think I must have gone to sleep almost right away. I don't remember anything until I was awakened by a strange buzzing noise.

I opened my eyes. The room was pitch black. But the *buzz . . . buzz . . . buzz* went on. It seemed to come from very close by. Then, I noticed a small light winking on and off on Brains' radio.

Brains was sitting up in bed.

"What's . . . what's wrong?" I asked groggily.

"Get up!" he said. His voice was sharp. "Hurry! It's the burglar alarm. Somebody is trying to break into the lab!"

CHAPTER 12

Daring Venture

I COULDN'T move. Honest, I couldn't.

Brains slung himself out of bed and began dressing hurriedly. The glow from the winking light on the radio made his face look like a scary Halloween mask.

"Hurry!" he whispered again.

I threw back the sheet and got up. Otto had tracked down Skeets. That seemed certain. And he was now forcing his way into the lab. The Joker would be with him. Maybe some more of his thugs, too. It was crazy for us to go out there. What could we do? How could we stop them?

"Brains," I said. "The police . . ."

"They wouldn't get here in time," he said. "This is up to us. Come on . . . Come on."

He reached over and snapped a switch on the radio. The buzzing stopped and the light went out.

My blue jeans lay crumpled on a chair where I'd tossed them. I pulled them over my pajamas but my hands were shaking so I had a hard time. I suddenly felt strangely cramped in the legs and I almost fell.

"What's wrong with you?" Brains asked, irritably. "Let's go!"

"My legs," I said. "Something's wrong with my legs."

He bent close to me, staring.

"You idiot," he said. "You've got your pants on back to front."

Creeps! I had.

"No time to change them now," he said. "Come on!"

He slipped like a shadow across the room to the open window. The night was pretty dark, yet there was enough moonlight coming in from outside for me to see him bend down and take an object from a wooden box on the floor. The object was big and roundish—like a small barrel.

He began to unwind something from it. And only then did I realize that the whole thing was a rolled-up rope ladder. He attached one end of the ladder to hooks under the sill and dropped the rest out the window.

I was startled. Brains had never told me about having a rope ladder. Creeps! We weren't going down by the house stairs—but by that thing.

Brains turned swiftly to me.

"Get a weapon!" he whispered tensely. "We're leaving."

I noticed for the first time that he was now holding what seemed to be a long metal flashlight. I hadn't seen him pick it up but I knew what it was. It was another of his inventions. The barrel was filled with sneezing powder. By pressing a button a jet of the powder could be sprayed into a person's face.

I almost threw my arm out of joint but I got my jeans fastened in the back. Then, I snatched up the first thing that looked like a weapon. It happened to be a baseball bat. I felt a little better with something hefty in my hands, but not much.

I slipped my feet into my sneakers and made for the window, sort of hobbling. I don't know if you've ever had your pants on backwards and tried to run. But it's strictly weird. You don't know if you're coming or going.

When I got to the window, Brains had already climbed over the sill and was starting down the ladder. I leaned out and watched. The ladder swayed against the ivy that covered the wall of the house and the hooks creaked.

Brains reached the bottom and looked up. His face was just a whitish blur. He motioned with his hand to me.

I didn't want to go down. But if Brains could do it, I sure could. The ladder shook under my weight. Or maybe it was just me. Anyway, I made it to the ground.

Brains was crouched in the shrubs that grew all along the back of the house. He was staring across the yard at the garage, sneezing powder gun at the ready. He put his finger over his lips in a gesture for silence.

Everything was very still. The only sound came from the rustling of a faint breeze through the big poplar tree nearby. I could see the front of the garage fairly clearly. The doors were closed and nobody seemed to be lurking there. But the side of the garage toward us was in heavy shadow from the lilac bushes. It was dark enough to hide Otto and the Joker and a half dozen more guys.

No lights showed through the upstairs windows of the lab. Skeets, of course, would know better than to turn any on. That is, if Skeets were still around and hadn't already been grabbed by Otto.

Brains stayed squatted, head thrust forward. I guess he was mapping out a campaign or something.

I knew that he had installed photoelectric cells at the front of the garage and at the sides and the rear, too. If any of the beams of invisible light were broken it would set off the burglar alarm. That meant that the prowler or prowlers could be anywhere around the building. Or they might have forced open the window at the back and got in that way.

Brains jabbed me with his elbow.

"We'll have to make a dash for it," he whispered.

He slid through the shrubs and started running across the lawn. I was right behind him. The grass was wet with dew and slippery. That, plus my fool back-to-front jeans almost tripped me up a couple of times.

But I reached the front of the garage O.K. and we dropped flat.

We stayed there, motionless, listening. I couldn't hear anything except the pounding of my heart.

After a moment, Brains rose to his feet and began sneaking along the front of the garage toward the corner of the building where the lilac bushes were so thick. I took a firmer grip on the baseball bat and followed.

When Brains gained the corner, he stopped so suddenly that I bumped into him.

"Shhhhh," he warned.

He peeked cautiously around the side. Apparently he didn't see anything suspicious because he made the turn along the north wall. I was so close behind I could have been his shadow.

Once again he crouched down. It was dark as pitch under the lilac bushes. Brains touched me and made a circling motion with his hand. I could barely see his gesture but I knew that he meant that we were to scout all the way around the garage.

He moved off, easing himself along. We had to be most careful now. Just the snap of a twig might bring our downfall. It was a horrible experience, I tell you, wondering where the intruders were, waiting with every nerve on edge.

Brains had worked his way almost to the secret entrance to the lab. I was a yard or so behind. Suddenly, I heard a rustling in the bushes back of me. Then, something cold and clammy touched my bare ankle.

At any other time I know I would have let out a yell. But I was beyond that. I was dumb with terror.

I forced myself to half turn around. And for a moment, I just couldn't believe what I saw.

A dog was there! Gulliver. Bimbo's little dog. He was looking up at me and wagging his tail and sort of whimpering.

"Brains!" I managed to gasp. "Look!"

Brains came back quickly. I think he was about to shoot blindly with his sneezing powder gun when he, too, saw Gulliver.

The little dog let out a couple of sharp barks and jumped up on Brains.

"Shhhh," Brains said. He patted Gulliver on the head. "Good dog. Good dog. Shhhh."

The barking stopped.

It had been Gulliver's cold nose that I'd felt on my ankle. I realized that now.

"How'd he get here?" I whispered.

"He must have run off from Bimbo and come looking for Skeets," Brains said.

That was it, of course. Bimbo had been afraid Gulliver might pull something like that.

"He was the one who probably set off the alarm," Brains said. "He could have easily passed between two of the photoelectric calls and interrupted the beam."

The tension that had been building up inside me let go. It was like sticking a pin into a balloon.

So it had been Gulliver who had caused all the excitement.

But to make sure, Brains and I, with the dog trotting behind us, circled the garage. We found nobody.

Brains had a key with him to the main doors of the garage and we went inside and up the stairs to the second floor. Brains gave the secret code knock. Even so, Skeets opened the door just an inch at first.

But when he saw who it was, he pushed it wide and we

went in. A small night light was burning and I noticed that Skeets had a heavy metal bar in his hand. He'd meant to make a fight of it if Otto had shown up.

Gulliver leaped all over Skeets while Brains explained what had happened. When he was through, Skeets fell back on his bed.

"I thought this was the payoff for sure," he said.

"You and a couple of other guys," I said.

I don't know exactly what made me go to one of the windows. Maybe I wanted to make doubly sure that Otto wasn't hanging around. Anyway, I pulled the curtain back a little and looked out.

Everything was darkish. Then, all of a sudden, a light went on in the Benton home.

"Brains!" I said. "The light's on in your parents' room!"

Brother, that did it.

Leaving Gulliver with Skeets, Brains and I made a jet-propelled exit. Even with the handicap of my reversed jeans, I beat Brains across the yard to the rope ladder. And the way I went up it would have made a sailor seasick with envy. Old X was no slouch, either.

Soon as we were in Brains' bedroom, we hauled in the ladder, flung it into the box and dived for our beds.

We weren't a second too soon. My head had barely hit the pillow when I heard footsteps out in the hall, then a tap on the door.

"Boys, are you all right? I thought I heard a noise."

It was Brains' mother.

Neither of us answered.

I kept my eyes open just a slit and I saw the door open.

Mrs. Benton looked in. Brains began breathing deeply, mixing it up with faint peanut whistle sounds.

We must have put it over O.K., for Mrs. Benton went out and closed the door. I heard her walk away down the hall.

Brains sat up in bed and began to change back to his pajamas.

"Well," he said, "this false alarm has taught me something."

I was struggling to get out of my jeans.

"It taught me plenty, too," I said. "Mainly, that even if you're in a rush, take time to get your pants on right."

"I don't mean that," Brains said. "I mean that we must remove this threat of Otto right away. He didn't come here tonight. But he might another night. There is only one way to stop him—find that missing paper. Tomorrow we shall take definite action."

"Such as?" I asked.

"I shall inform you of my plan in the morning," Brains said. "In the meantime, get plenty of rest, Operative Three. Unless I am mistaken, you are going to need it."

Then, he stretched out full length, turned over on his side and closed his eyes.

CHAPTER 13

Risky Scheme

THE next morning when we got up, Brains still wouldn't give me the low down.

"First I must consult with Skeets," he said. "Curb your impatience, Operative Three. You shall know the details in good time."

There was no sense hammering at him. That would only make him clam up more. So, I acted as if I couldn't have cared less. But, frankly, I was leery of what he was up to. Anything that had to do with finding the missing paper could bring a load of grief.

And, as it turned out, how right I was!

When we got downstairs, we found that Mrs. Ray had been up since dawn and was about to take off for her sister's home upstate. She was to be gone for two days but from the way she dithered you'd think she was leaving for the moon with a side trip to Mars.

Mr. Benton finally drove her to the bus station and everybody sort of breathed a sigh of relief. I know Brains and I did. It was going to be tough enough keeping Skeets' presence in the garage a secret, especially now that Gulliver had arrived. And we sure could do without Mrs. Ray's extra-good eyes and ears.

Brains' mother didn't mention that she'd come to our room during the night. So I guess she figured she'd imagined hearing the noise that had awakened her. But she did tell us not to eat breakfast so fast.

"My goodness," she said. "You'd think this was the last meal you'd ever have. Why the rush?"

"We are busy on a project," Brains said.

We hit for the lab while Mrs. Benton was working on her second cup of coffee. As we passed through the kitchen Brains sneaked a couple of cans of something from the back of one of the shelves. I didn't find out what it was until we got outside.

"Dog food for Gulliver," he whispered as we crossed the yard. "Left over from when we had Curly."

Curly was Brains' airedale who had died of old age about half a year ago.

Skeets was just getting up when we walked in and he was still sleepy. But not Gulliver. He gave us a noisy welcome. So did the Senator.

We got them both piped down as fast as we could by feeding them. Then, Brains started quizzing Skeets. I was all ears.

"Skeets," he said, "I'm convinced that your father did not hide the vital document in the trunk or its contents. Now, think hard. Did you bring any other item of your father's with you when you left the circus?"

"No," Skeets said. "That was all."

"But he must have left other possessions," Brains went on.

"Oh, sure. Plenty of stuff."

"For instance . . ."

"All the circus equipment and the animals and . . ."

Brains cut him off. "I mean personal things that were his and his alone. Can you think of anything that your father used frequently that still remains at the circus?"

Skeets frowned.

"Well, let's see now . . ."

Brains bent forward. "Did he have a desk?"

"Yes," Skeets said. "Of course he did. He used it every day, working on the circus business and his own private things."

"Ah," Brains murmured. "And is Otto using that desk now?"

Skeets nodded. "He took it over when he became manager."

"Does this desk always go along when the circus is on the road?"

"Yes."

"Where was it when you saw it last?" Brains asked.

"In Otto's private office on the circus train."

"Does he always have his office on the train?"

"No," Skeets said. "In some places there is office space right on the lot. In that case, the desk and the business records are moved there, especially if the engagement is for more than a day or so."

"What about in Middlebury?"

Skeets thought for a moment. "Middlebury . . . The circus uses the fair grounds at Middlebury. There is a small building with a couple of offices in it that's turned over to the management."

I had been standing there, looking from one to the other like somebody watching a tennis match. But I was beginning to get a horrible idea.

"What does this desk look like?" Brains asked.

"It's just an ordinary business desk. Flat top. Two rows of drawers. Beat-up looking."

"Is there anything distinctive about it?" Brains asked. "I mean some feature that would enable a person to recognize it right away?"

Skeets ran his fingers through his hair. The brown powder that Bimbo had put on was wearing off and blond streaks showed.

"I don't think so . . ." He stopped suddenly and snapped his fingers. "Of course, there is. Each of the drawers has a clown's head as a handle—just like the one on the trunk."

"Good," Brains said. He seemed pleased.

Skeets eyed him. "Why the third-degree?"

Brains picked up the book he had been reading the night before, *Solutions of Puzzling Crime Cases*. He tapped it with a forefinger.

"During my research in this volume I found that, in two of these cases, missing documents were located stacked away in secret desk drawers. I have a feeling that your father might have done likewise."

Skeets' eyes brightened. "Say, maybe you're right. All of my father's private papers were removed before Otto took over. But I don't think Bimbo ever examined the desk for a secret drawer."

I decided to get into the act before this thing got too far out of hand.

"Look," I said. "If the paper *is* hidden in that desk, so what? We haven't a chance of even looking for it, let alone finding it. It might as well be on the top of Mount Everest."

"There are always ways and means to investigate even the most guarded objects," Brains said.

He walked briskly across the lab and pressed the button of the private telephone to his house.

Mrs. Benton's voice sounded almost immediately from the wall speaker.

"Is that you, son?"

"Yes, mother," Brains said into the microphone. "Jimmy and I would like to attend the circus this afternoon. It's playing at Middlebury. We could go by bus and be back in time for dinner. Have you any objections?"

"Why, no, dear," Mrs. Benton said. "I think that would be a nice change for both of you."

"One other thing," Brains said. "Could you advance me some money on my allowance, Mother? Say four or five dollars? That would be enough—with what I have."

"Very well. I'll leave it on the kitchen table. Your father

has just returned from the bus station and we're off for the college. Have fun."

"Thank you, Mother," Brains said.

Have fun, she'd said. *Fun!* Creeps!

Brains turned to us.

"Well, gentlemen," he said. "How does the proposition sound to you?"

Skeets looked as if somebody had slugged him.

"You don't honestly mean you're going to Middlebury and search that desk?" he said. "You're kidding."

"Of course, we're going," Brains said. "Nothing daunts the Benton and Carson International Detective Agency."

"But you won't stand a ghost of a chance," Skeets said. "There'll be people around. Otto, himself, might be there, and the Joker."

"We can at least survey the situation," Brains said.

He glanced at me.

"You seem rather pale, Operative Three. You *do* need a change of scene . . . Now let us get busy. There are several things that must be attended to before our departure. While I am in the house collecting the funds, take Gulliver out into the lane and exercise him thoroughly so that he will not need to repeat the performance until our return. If anyone should see you and ask about Gulliver, merely say that we're keeping the dog for a friend."

Brains started for the lab door, then he stopped.

"Another thing," he said. "You had better make some arrangement for a substitute to deliver your newspapers. In case we are . . . ah . . . detained. You should be able to do that by telephone. As I recall it, Stinky Green has done this chore for you before . . . And, oh yes, instruct him not to bother about the Madden house. You can take a newspaper to Bimbo, yourself, later."

Well, like I told you, I'd been leery all along of what Brains was cooking up. But, even so, I'd never figured that it would be a crazy stunt like this. Why nobody in their right mind would think of calmly walking into Otto's office and looking through his desk.

Did I put my foot down and refuse to have any part of the scheme? Did I tell Brains that if he wanted to go and get himself beaten up and maybe shot, he could darn well do it alone?

Of course, I told him. I didn't pull any punches.

But when the ten o'clock bus left Crestwood and headed up the highway for Middlebury, Brains was on it.

And so was I.

CHAPTER 14

Objective Sighted

O F COURSE, I should have saved my breath sounding off like that to Brains. He knew I'd go along no matter how I beefed. And I guess I knew it too, deep down inside. In fact, I think that if he'd taken me at my word and started to leave me behind, I would've socked him.

That didn't mean that I liked this haywire scheme any better. Suppose we did get into Otto's office and examined the desk. What would happen if we were caught? We could be arrested. Or Otto might . . . Creeps, there was no telling *what* he might do.

I don't know if you've ever driven over the highway

from Crestwood to the city of Middlebury but the scenery is supposed to be very special. "Picturesque" is the word my mother uses. The road winds through wooded hills and goes right past Lake Carmine where the fishing's so good. Except for a few cottages and hunting lodges scattered around, the whole district is pretty wild looking.

But I was in no mood to appreciate scenic wonders during that bus ride. I was as wound up as an alarm clock at midnight.

Brains, however, didn't seem the least bit jittery. He sat there beside me, wearing that bird-dog look of his. Sort of bright-eyed and straining at the leash as if he just couldn't wait. He's plain nuts when he's on the trail of anything, whether it's an invention or taking a test at school or chasing a funny-colored butterfly.

It was noon when we arrived at the terminal in downtown Middlebury. Brains and I got out to transfer to a local bus that would take us to the fair grounds. But there were so many kids and grownups heading for the same place that we had to line up.

You see, the annual Middlebury Fair was on as well as the circus and the two things were really pulling the crowds.

About everywhere you looked were signs advertising the big events. The largest and splashiest were posters of roaring lions and twirling acrobats and sword-swallowers and freaks. Lettered in bright red on each was: *THE GREAT AND MAGNIFICENT FENTON CIRCUS Bigger and Better Than Ever*. And at the bottom: Otto P. R. Gruber, *President and Manager*.

We finally pushed our way onto a packed city bus and got to the fair grounds. Even though the afternoon had barely begun, the place was already jumping with noise and people and excitement.

You know what it's like—the air filled with wonderful smells of hamburgers frying and popcorn popping; guys yelling at you to buy a souvenir or a hot dog or ice cream; the ground littered with peanut shells and empty cracker-jack boxes; the Midway's giant Ferris wheel going round and round; the sound of brassy music; and, in the distance, the booming swish of cars racing like crazy bugs up and down the tracks of the roller-coaster.

It was all there. But what I saw mainly was the big central tent of the Fenton Circus with a circle of smaller tents around it.

"We're early," Brains said. "The afternoon performance doesn't start until two-fifteen. That's when I'm counting on Otto to leave his office. We'll have time now to scout around and find the building Skeets described."

"First let's eat," I said.

Brains had no objections so we bought hot dogs and munched them as we walked along. In a little while we came to a large signpost with arrows pointing this way and that. One of the arrows was lettered: BUSINESS OFFICE, FENTON CIRCUS.

The butterflies in my stomach began to test their wings.

The Middlebury fair grounds is quite a layout with some paved streets and a few permanent buildings. We turned along the street indicated by the arrow and it took us right by the main circus tent. It was too early for customers but an attendant was loafing by the ticket booth with a batch of programs under his arm. I was surprised when Brains went up and bought one.

"What's the big idea?" I asked as we moved away. "We aren't going in to see the show."

Brains was busily leafing through the program.

"No, indeed we aren't," he said. "But you must remember that even though you caught a glimpse of a man you took to be Otto Gruber, we do not know precisely what he looks like. I hope to remedy that right now."

He suddenly stopped turning the pages.

"Ah," he said. "I was sure such a person would have his picture prominently displayed. Look here."

Brains held up the open program for me to see.

A photograph of a beefy-faced man occupied most of one of the pages. He had small dark eyes and a wide, thin-lipped mouth. Maybe he'd been trying to smile for the photographer but it looked more like a sneer to me.

Under the photograph was printed:

Otto P. R. Gruber
President and Manager of the Fenton Circus

After the tragic death of Alfred B. Fenton, founder and president of the Fenton Circus, the reins of office were taken over by Otto P. R. Gruber. Born in Torrance, Pennsylvania, Mr. Gruber has long had a keen interest in the thrills and glamour of the Big Top. Sportsman and ardent fisherman, the new president has used all his abilities and enthusiasms to now present to the public the greatest spectacle that the Fenton Circus has ever produced.

Brains seemed to be taking a long time staring at the page. I began to get restless.

"That's odd," he muttered. "I thought from what Bimbo said that Otto had been born in England, as Skeets' parents had. Not here in the U.S."

"The trouble is that he was ever born at all," I said. "And by the way, he's the guy I saw in the car that day, I'm sure of it."

Brains folded the program and stuck it in his pocket.

"Well, now that we know what he looks like," he said, "we can be on the alert. The next step is to locate the office and put it under surveillance. Come along."

We walked quite a distance, away from the stands and attractions. The noise of the Midway had dwindled to a murmur when we reached a section of the fair grounds that had grass and flower beds and trees. There were benches scattered around and some drinking fountains. It was like a park.

Suddenly Brains touched my arm.

"There," he said.

I had seen the low frame building the moment he spoke. It stood back from the roadway with a clipped hedge on either side. The building was one-story and smallish. It looked like a cottage where people might live. A sign on a stake read: OFFICE OF FENTON CIRCUS.

But I didn't need the sign to know that we'd found what we were after. For parked in front of the building was a car of foreign make. It was the bright blue convertible I had seen Otto and the Joker in the other afternoon.

"That's Otto's car," I whispered to Brains. "He must be inside."

"So I have surmised," Brains said. He motioned toward

a bench on a pathway nearby. "We'll sit down there. Act as if you are tired and need to rest."

As soon as we were settled on the bench, Brains took the circus program from his pocket and opened it.

"If anybody comes out, pretend you're very interested in this magazine," he said. "We must do nothing to attract attention to ourselves. Otto might go out to lunch. In that event, we may be able to put our plan into operation sooner than I thought."

I'll swear Brains hadn't finished talking for more than a couple of seconds when the door of the building opened and two men came out. One was heavily built with wide shoulders and a big face. The other was taller and slimmer. He was wearing a black hat and he was smoking a cigar.

My heart gave a triple leap. I didn't need any crystal ball to know that the beefy man was Otto Gruber. He had on the same yellow sport coat I'd seen him wear before. And the man with him couldn't be anybody else but the Joker.

"Brains . . ." I started to gasp out.

He dug an elbow into my ribs. "Shhhhh," he whispered.

He held the circus program up in front of him. But I knew that he was looking over the top of it.

The play-acting wasn't necessary. We were pretty far away, and anyway Otto and the Joker didn't even notice us. They got into the blue convertible and drove off in the direction of the circus tents.

We waited until the car was out of sight, then Brains stood up.

"There is not a moment to lose," he said tensely. "This is our chance."

"Now wait a minute," I said. "How do we know somebody else isn't in that office?"

"An able detective meets situations as they arise," he said. "If we do meet anyone and are questioned, here is our story. We are reporters from our school paper. We are doing research for an article on circus life."

"During summer vacation?" I said.

"We are working on the fall issue," Brains said. "Be ready with pad and pencil so it will look as if you've been taking notes."

I felt in my pockets.

"I haven't got a pad *or* a pencil," I said.

Brains was always so prepared for everything that it annoyed him when other people weren't. He ripped off some sheets from a pad he had and handed them to me.

"I have only one pencil and I'll need that myself," he said. "Perhaps we'll be able to find you one when we get inside . . . Now let's move. We must make our approach seem casual. So just saunter."

Saunter! Creeps, I'd be lucky if I could walk at all.

CHAPTER 15

The Search

WE went along the roadway, then up the path that led to the building. Talk about your last mile.

Maybe Brains was as tense as I was, but he sure didn't show it. He just ambled along, nice and easy, sort of whistling to himself and shuffling his big feet. He made a perfect picture of a not-too-bright kid who had wandered off from the fair.

As I said before, this building was like a one-story small house. There were windows in the front with flowers growing in boxes and green shutters. The door was toward the side, near the corner.

One of the windows was open and from it I heard the *click-click-click* of a typewriter. We were close enough now for me to get a look through the window. Inside was a large room furnished like an office with desks and filing cabinets. And seated at a desk, halfway down the room, was a blonde-haired woman. Her back was to us and she was hammering away at a typewriter. She seemed to be alone.

"Brains," I whispered, when we reached the front door. "It's no use. There's somebody in there. We'd better beat it."

"No indeed," he said. "We aren't interested in the office where the typist is—but in Otto's private one."

The front door had a large glass panel. Brains put his face close to it and peered through.

"And that may be it," he said, excitedly. "Down there at the end of the hall!"

I, too, looked through the glass. Beyond was a narrow hallway that ran almost the full depth of the building. At one side of this hall was a closed door which I figured led to the office where the woman was typing. A second door, the one Brains meant, was at the far end. It was closed, too, and on it was lettered: PRIVATE.

"We can't go down there," I said. "She's sure to hear us."

"With all that clatter?" Brains said. "You stay here while I reconnoiter."

He opened the front door and slipped inside. I watched him tiptoe down the hall. I expected the sound of typing to stop and the woman to come out of the big office. But the clicking of the keys went on.

It took Brains only a moment or so to reach the door

marked PRIVATE. Maybe he knocked a couple of times to make sure nobody was inside. I couldn't tell from where I was. But I did see him grasp the doorknob and cautiously push the door part way open.

He took a quick look. Then, he turned and beckoned frantically for me to come.

Well, I went, but the butterflies in my stomach were really looping the loop now.

"It's Otto's office," Brains whispered when I joined him.

"Are you sure?" I asked.

I stuck my head in. The room was small and it seemed crowded with a desk, a couple of chairs and a bookcase. But I wasn't interested in the furniture, except for one item —the desk. It was battered and scarred and looked as if it had been kicked around a lot. One thing made it different from any ordinary office desk—the handles on the drawers.

Each handle was made of brass and was modeled in the form of a clown's head, exactly the same as the one on Skeets' trunk.

It *was* Otto's desk—the one Skeets had described!

"Stay here in the hall," Brains whispered. "I'm going in. Keep your eyes on the front door. If anybody comes, tip me off."

He slid past me into the office before I could say anything.

There was nothing for me to do but stand there by the doorway to Otto's private office and shiver. I had a pretty good view of the roadway through the glass in the front door. And I'd probably be able to sight anyone just before they came into the building. Even so, we wouldn't have a chance of getting away if anyone *did* come.

I think I aged so much in the next few minutes I was eligible for the draft. Every once in a while I shifted my eyes from the front door to see how Brains was doing. He was working like mad over the desk, pulling out drawers and feeling around inside where they'd been. He was probing for a secret panel where the paper might be hidden. But he sure didn't seem to be having any luck.

All the time the sound of the typing in the next office kept up. I was thankful for that. But at any moment the woman might get through and come out into the hall. And then we'd be in the soup up to our crew-cuts.

A couple of cars drove by on the road. One was a foreign job sort of like Otto's and I thought for sure he and the Joker had come back. But it turned out to be a false alarm.

Brains had put the drawers back in place and he now ducked down to examine the underside of the desk. There was a lot of fishing equipment, rods and stuff, stacked in one corner of the office. I suppose it belonged to Otto. The write-up in the circus program had said he was a hot-shot fisherman.

I don't know exactly how it happened. Brains must have hit the equipment with his foot when he crawled under the desk. Anyway, the whole works, rods and all, fell crashing to the floor.

Brother, what a noise! I was sure the racket would bring the typist tearing out of her office to find out what had happened. But the *click-click-click* went on without even a pause. She sure must have had a whale of a lot of letters to type.

I was trying to get my heart beat back to somewhere near

normal when I saw a man walking up the path from the street. He was heading straight for the front door.

"Brains!" I gasped. "Somebody's coming."

Brains was under the desk but he rolled free and sprang to his feet almost in one motion. There was no time to pick up the fallen fishing equipment.

"Get out your note paper," he snapped.

He lunged for the open door. But as he swung around the desk, he reached out and grabbed up a pencil that was lying there and handed it to me. Even in an emergency he didn't forget a detail like that.

Brains had just closed the door of the office behind him when the man came into the building. We were trapped.

"Don't give your right name," Brains muttered out of the side of his mouth.

"What'll I use?" I whispered.

"Any name. The first one you think of."

The man started down the hall, walking heavily. He was a big, tough-looking guy, wearing blue jeans and a black sweater. I tagged him as one of the circus' roustabouts.

Brains now had his pad out and was going through the motions of writing something on it. I followed his example, using the pencil he'd given me.

It was sort of dark at the end of the hall where we were and the man didn't notice us until he was halfway down the corridor. Suddenly he caught sight of us.

"What're you kids doin' here?" he said.

He kept on coming, walking faster.

"Good afternoon," Brains said smoothly. "Perhaps you can help us, sir."

The guy came to a stop in front of us, head thrust forward, his arms sort of dangling. The sleeves of his sweater were rolled up. His arms were hairy and bulging with muscle. He was the type with a low I.Q. but a high K.O.

"Whatcha mean help you," he demanded.

"Well," Brains said. "You see my friend and I are doing research. We hope to write an article for our school paper on life in the circus."

"Yeah?" the guy said. "Well, whatcha hangin' around here for?"

"We are seeking background material," Brains went on. "Everybody knows about the wild animals and the aerial acts. But we would like to get some information on the administration of a circus. Is the manager in?"

Brother, could he reel off the hokum.

"Nah," the man said. "And he don't like kids snoopin' around either . . . What's your name?"

He jabbed a finger the size of a small banana at Brains.

"John Quincy Adams," Brains said.

The guy sort of squinted.

"John . . . what?"

"Quincy," Brains said. "Q as in quixotic or quadruped . . . Quincy Adams. A as in anthropoid or ape . . ."

"A'right . . . a'right," the man growled. He seemed to be trying to memorize the name.

Then he turned to me.

"What's yours, buster?"

I couldn't think of any name. I just couldn't. I was so scared my mind went blank. Has it ever happened to you? I mean, say you're going to introduce somebody to somebody else and all of a sudden you sort of black out in the head. Well, that's the way it was with me.

"C'mon . . . c'mon," the guy said.

I tried to think of something . . . anything. Give any name, Brains had said.

"Let's have it," the man said. He was suspicious now. "Your name."

"Brains Benton," I gasped out.

Brains sort of stiffened as if I'd plunged a dagger into his back.

I could have choked myself gladly. I don't know why I'd come out with that.

"Brains Benton," the man repeated. "You think I'm gonna believe a phony name like that. Why . . ."

The sound of the front door opening cut him off. He turned and looked down the hall. So did Brains. So did I.

And I almost passed dead away.

Two men had come into the building. One was broad-shouldered and stocky looking. The other was tall and thinnish.

I didn't have to look twice to know that the men were Otto and the Joker!

CHAPTER 16

Getaway

I HEARD Brains draw in his breath with a sort of *sssss* sound. I was too paralyzed to do even that.

Otto saw us.

"Pete!" he called. "Who's that with you?"

"Couple of kids, Mr. Gruber," the roustabout character said. "I found 'em snoopin' around."

"What do they want?" Otto asked.

He and the Joker were almost on us now.

"They claim they're writin' somethin' for a school newspaper," Pete said. "On th' circus."

Otto and the Joker stopped about a yard away. They

both stared at us hard and their expressions were tough and mean. Scared as I was I noticed how decked out Otto was with jewelry made in the form of the clown's head. His tie clasp had the clown on it. So did the big brass buckle on his belt. And he was wearing a gold clown-head ring, too.

"Did they swipe anything?" the Joker asked.

He had a big cigar stuck in his mouth and his voice was rasping and foreign sounding.

"Naw," Pete said. "I saw 'em before they got into th' office here."

"Good thing," Otto said. "I forgot to lock it. That's why we came back."

He kept staring at us.

"You see that sign on the door?" he said. "It says Private and it means private. Understand?"

"Yes, sir," Brains said. "We were just trying to get some information . . ."

"Well, clear out!" Otto said. "I have no time . . . Clear out before I call the police and have you run in."

"Yes, sir," Brains said.

"Yes, sir," I said.

We bumped into each other in our eagerness to get up the hall to the front door. Brother, did we make tracks.

Just before we reached the door I heard the Joker say, "You know, Otto, those kids . . . I think I've seen 'em some place before. That short one, especially . . . But I can't figure where."

"Did you get their names, Pete?"

That was Otto speaking.

Brains pushed the front door open. As we scooted out I heard Pete say,

"Yeah. One of 'em was . . ."

The door closed behind us and I didn't hear any more.

"Run!" Brains said. "Fast as you can!"

We didn't go down the path. We cut across the grass to the roadway. Otto's car was parked there. We sprinted past it and headed for the fair.

Suddenly a voice yelled from behind us.

"Hey! You kids! Come back here!"

It was the Joker.

We kept on going, turning on extra speed. We rounded a bend in the road and were out of sight of the building. Not too far ahead of us was the Midway with its sideshows and throngs of people.

"Hurry!" Brains panted. "Our only chance is to lose ourselves in the crowd."

We did just that. But, I tell you, I had more than one anxious moment before we were dodging through the mob.

"Let's catch a bus and get out of here," I said.

"Yes," Brains replied. "The sooner the better."

We finally reached the place where the buses for downtown Middlebury loaded and we scrambled aboard one.

"Why on earth did you give my name?" Brains asked when we found a seat.

"I don't know," I said miserably. "I was so rattled I just couldn't think what to tell him."

"Well, I hope no harm's done," Brains said. "But I'm afraid the Joker recognized us . . . you, in particular. Don't forget, he and Otto got a good look at you the afternoon they called at the Madden house. Do you remember?"

I nodded. Both Otto and the Joker *had* given me the once-over as they'd driven past that afternoon.

"Even so," I said. "I was just a kid delivering newspapers. They wouldn't link me up with Skeets."

"Not unless the Joker remembered seeing you once before—in the field when we came to Skeets' rescue."

"But they won't be able to trace me," I said. "They don't know my name."

"They know mine," Brains said.

I'm sure I went a little pale. I should have, the way I felt. My stupid mistake in blurting out Brains' name could get us into trouble. Real trouble.

Brains slumped back in the seat.

"The whole afternoon's been a complete fiasco," he said. "My theory that we might find a secret compartment in the desk turning out to be a failure . . . and now this."

I wanted desperately to get clear away and back to Crestwood. But the bus seemed to take forever to get going. I guess the driver was ahead of schedule for he was loafing around outside, smoking a cigarette and gabbing with a couple of guys. Finally, he looked at his watch and got back of the wheel.

We had just begun to roll down the highway when Brains looked out the window and gave me a jab.

"Duck," he said. "Quick!"

I did. Out of the corner of my eye as I went down, I got a glimpse of a car speeding past the bus. It was Otto's blue foreign job. Otto was driving and the Joker was beside him. They had fishing rods and stuff sticking out the back.

For a moment, I thought they might be going to stop the bus and see if we were on it. But the car went streaking ahead.

I looked at Brains.

"I wonder where they're going?" I said.

"I wish I knew," he said. "Maybe they are off to do some fishing. They have the equipment along."

When we reached downtown Middlebury, we had to wait twenty minutes for a bus to Crestwood. And it was way past three-thirty when we hit town.

We lit out for Brains' place, almost running. On the way I saw Stinky Green, the kid I'd got to take over my paper route. He'd just come from the *Ledger* office and had a delivery bag packed full of the afternoon editions.

"Hey!" he said, surprised to see me. "I thought you were going to be away all afternoon."

"So did I," I said. "But I got back sooner than I expected. I still want you to do the job, only give me one paper for the Madden house. I'll take that out myself."

He took a rolled up paper from his bag and flipped it to me. I stuck it in my hip pocket.

"Come on, Jimmy," Brains said.

"Say, Brains," Stinky said. "Was that some relative of yours who called at your house in the snazzy foreign car?"

"What foreign car?" Brains said.

"I saw a nifty job turn in your driveway about an hour ago," Stinky said. "Man, what a wagon."

"What color was it?" Brains asked sharply.

I held my breath.

"Blue," Stinky said. "Why?"

Brains didn't answer. Neither did I. We left Stinky stand-ing there with his mouth open and sprinted on. It wasn't far to Brains' house but it seemed to take forever to get there.

As we raced down the drive, I saw that one of the garage doors was open. The wind was swinging it back and forth. We had left both doors closed, and locked.

Oh, no, I thought. Please not that.

Brains went into the garage with me right behind him. At the back, the door to the lab at the top of the steps was also open.

We took the steps two at a time and burst into the lab. I could hear the Senator screaming,

"Cut his throat! Cut his throat!"

"Skeets!" Brains called. "Skeets!"

The parrot was there, fluttering around on his perch in the isolation booth. But there was no sign of anyone else in the place.

The little dog, Gulliver, had vanished. And so had Skeets!

CHAPTER 17

The Clue

WE LOOKED everywhere, yelling Skeets' name. But it was no use.

I felt as if the whole world had come crashing down on us.

"They've got him!" I said. "I don't know how . . . but they've got him!"

"Now wait a minute," Brains said. "We can't be sure. We have no proof."

"No proof!" I let out. "With Stinky seeing a blue foreign car turn in the drive and with Skeets gone! What do you want—a recorded statement?"

"There are many foreign cars painted blue," Brains said.

"And they all drive up to your house. Come on. We can't waste time hanging around here. Let's do something."

I didn't know exactly what . . . but something, anything.

"Hold on," Brains said. "Hold on. We must use our heads."

He started in on that pacing act of his and I knew it was useless to try to hurry him.

The Senator had been squawking like crazy in the isolation booth since we'd come in. I got some sunflower seeds and dumped them in his cup. I didn't do it to shut him up. With Brains' parents and Mrs. Ray away, the parrot could scream his throat out. I just had to keep busy or I'd flip, that was all.

"There's one thing that baffles me," Brains said. "If Otto and the Joker did come here, how did they get into the garage and the lab? We left all the doors locked and they haven't been forced open. Skeets certainly wouldn't have unlocked the doors and let in those two men . . . And what about Gulliver? Where has he gone?"

It was a puzzler, I had to admit. But it didn't seem to matter. Not now, anyway.

"I don't know the answers," I said. "You're the guy who figures those things. Maybe Otto and the Joker tricked Skeets into coming outside and then they grabbed him. Maybe they kidnapped Gulliver, too . . . I don't know."

Brains looked at me sharply.

"You may have hit on something," he said.

He turned and hurried back down the stairs. He was

examining the driveway in front of the garage when I joined him.

"A car was here, all right," Brains said.

He pointed to an oil stain on the gravel of the drive.

"It parked long enough for the dripping from a leak to accumulate. My parents won't be home until after six tonight, so it wasn't our car."

Brains walked a couple of yards closer to the garage. I saw him look down at a place in the drive where the gravel seemed to have been sort of kicked around.

"A scuffle may have occurred here," he said.

"You mean that's where Skeets was grabbed . . . and he put up a fight."

"A possibility, anyway," Brains said.

He dropped down on his knees and began inspecting that part of the drive. I watched him run his fingers over the bits of gravel. Suddenly his hand darted forward and he picked up something.

"What'd you find?" I asked excitedly.

"This," he said.

He held out his hand. In his palm was a tie clip with a piece of cloth attached to it. It was no ordinary clip. It was made in the shape of a clown's head.

"Otto's!" I gasped.

"Yes, Otto's," Brains said. "Skeets undoubtedly tried to get away from him and in the struggle he must have ripped the clip from Otto's tie."

Brains came quickly to his feet.

"It is all the proof we need," he said. "You were right. Jimmy. They *have* got him."

I'd been positive of it from the start. Just as I'd been positive about something else . . . something I didn't like to think about.

"Brains," I began and I had a hard time putting into words what I had to say. "Did they know to come here because . . . because I gave your name?"

"I'm afraid that could have done it, Jimmy," he said. "If the Joker remembered where he'd seen us, that would connect us with Skeets. And they'd try to track us down in order to find him. All they had to do was look up the name Benton in the Crestwood telephone directory—and there's only one Benton in the book—copy down the address, and drive here. Simplicity itself."

I winced. I'd sure made a mess of things. Creeps!

"What're we going to do?" I said. I was desperate.

"Find Skeets somehow and get him back," Brains said.

"But how? *How?*"

Brains ran his fingers through his hair. He took a step toward the garage and stopped. He seemed flustered and undecided.

"I honestly don't know, Jimmy," he said.

It was a shock to hear him say that. I mean he was so smart and had so much savvy I naturally expected him to come up with all the answers. I found it hard, at times, to remember that he was not much older than I was.

"We'd better go out and talk to Bimbo and the Queen," Brains said. "Maybe they'll have an idea where Otto might have taken Skeets . . . Get the bikes, Jimmy, while I lock up the lab and the garage. And hurry!"

We both sailed into action and within three minutes we

were on our bikes and making for the Madden house. It was a terrible ride out there, I tell you. I kept wondering and worrying about where Skeets was and what was happening to him. But the awful part was feeling it was all my fault.

As luck would have it, the rear tire of my bike went flat as we were turning up the lane to the Madden house.

"Go on ahead," I told Brains. "I'll have to walk."

When I reached the house, Brains was in the kitchen with Bimbo and the Queen. He had already given them the low-down on what had happened and the shock from the bad news still showed on their faces. But what surprised me was that the dog, Gulliver, was there.

"He appeared about half an hour ago," Bimbo said when I asked him about Gulliver. "He'd been gone since last night. I thought that he'd run off to find Skeets. But when he showed up I didn't know what to think."

Bimbo still had a patch of tape on his forehead and his eye looked blacker and puffier than before. But the Queen seemed even worse off. She was so upset she was almost shaking.

We all had a council of war around the kitchen table. Bimbo was positive that Otto wouldn't take Skeets back to the circus.

"Too many people might see the boy," Bimbo said, "and start asking questions. No, Otto's sure to keep him out of sight."

"But isn't there danger that Otto might eliminate Skeets for good and all?" Brains asked.

The Queen shuddered.

"Don't talk like that," she said.

Bimbo reached out and patted her hand.

"Now . . . now, Cleo," he said. "Otto wouldn't dare kill Skeets."

"He tried as much before when he had Skeets work out on the high trapeze, didn't he?" Brains said.

"Having him fall off a trapeze could be easily explained as an unfortunate accident," Bimbo said. "But having Skeets meet death away from the circus is quite another thing. It would be too risky for Otto. He wouldn't want to chance an investigation."

"I see," Brains said.

"Anyway," Bimbo went on, "I'm almost certain, from things I overheard when Otto and the Joker were here, that Otto believes Skeets has an idea where the secret paper is hidden. In fact I gathered that he believes Skeets ran away from the circus because he'd found the paper. If this is true, then Otto has taken Skeets to some out-of-the-way place to try to make him talk."

"Have you an idea where this place might be?" Brains asked.

Bimbo shook his head.

"Not the slightest. Except that I'm sure Otto would keep within fairly easy driving distance of the circus so he could go back and forth."

Brains sort of nodded.

"That means that Skeets is being held somewhere not too far from Middlebury. Have you a map of the area?"

"I've a roadmap of the state," Bimbo said.

He got it from a cupboard and Brains spread the map out on the table.

"Let's see," he murmured, bending over it. "Where's the highway between Middlebury and Crestwood . . .?"

Maybe my eyes are a little sharper than Brains'. Anyway, I spotted it right away. I got out the pencil we'd taken from Otto's office and put the point on the line marking the highway.

"Here," I said.

"Good," Brains said.

He took the pencil from me and began moving the point along the highway, following its winding course past Lake Carmine.

"I believe we can safely assume that Otto and the Joker followed this route from Middlebury to Crestwood when they came looking for Skeets at my home," he said.

"Check," I said.

All traffic between Middlebury and Crestwood used this highway. There were other roads but they were narrow backcountry things, full of holes and half the time washed out. They'd wreck a low-slung car like Otto's.

"All right," Brains went on. "Then the question now is, where did they go after they seized Skeets?"

"I think they'd head north, back toward Middlebury," Bimbo replied. "As I said before, Otto wouldn't want to be too far away from the circus."

"I agree," the Queen said.

She had got out her playing cards and was putting a number of them, face up, on the table.

"But if they *did* head north," Brains said, "it would have been about the time Jimmy and I were on the bus returning home to Crestwood. We didn't see Otto and the Joker pass

us on the highway. And I'm sure we would have spotted that blue car."

Bimbo leaned forward and studied the map.

"They could have turned off the highway before your bus came along," he said. "Maybe somewhere around this big lake."

"That's Lake Carmine," I said.

I began to get an idea.

"Hey," I said. "That would be a nifty place to hide out. There's nothing much around there but a few cottages and fishing lodges."

"Fishing lodges!" Brains said.

He looked at me and there was a kind of shiny light in his eyes.

"Isn't Otto supposed to be a great fisherman, Bimbo?" Brains asked.

"Yes, indeed," Bimbo said. "That's about the only good trait he has. I remember back in the old days he used to make Skeets' father wild the way he'd take time off to go fishing. Why, if the circus was playing near a lake or a good trout stream, Otto sometimes even rented a cottage so he could fish every spare moment."

"Maybe he did just that when the circus moved to Middlebury," Brains said.

"He might well have," Bimbo said.

"Lake Carmine would be the place he'd pick," I said. "It's the best fishing spot in miles."

I sat up straight as I suddenly remembered something.

"Brains!" I said. "Otto and the Joker had fishing tackle and stuff in their car. Remember?"

"Yes, Jimmy," Brains said quietly. "I do remember."

Bimbo whistled in a soft kind of way.

"I think we've got something," he said. "If Otto had a fishing lodge it would be a perfect out-of-the-way place to take Skeets."

"Made to order," Brains said.

"That's it!" I said. Man, I was so excited I almost yelled it. "That's the answer. Now all we have to do is find the lodge."

"It's not quite that simple, Jimmy," Brains said. "Even if we've guessed right, we still have a problem. You know the size of Lake Carmine. It would take us days to canvass all of the cottages and the lodges around those shores."

He moved the point of the pencil in a big circle over the Lake Carmine on the map.

"If we could only somehow determine in what section this fishing lodge might be," Brains said. "We would have a chance to . . ."

He gave a kind of gasp and stopped talking. I looked at him, startled. Brains was holding the pencil up in front of him and staring at it as if the thing had turned into solid uranium.

"Hey," I said, "what's biting you?"

"Isn't this the pencil I got from Otto's desk?" he asked.

"Sure it is," I said. "Why?"

"Look here," Brains said. He held out the pencil for us to see. "Look at this lettering!"

I leaned closer. Stamped in red on the side of the white pencil was: *The MacNab Real Estate Co., Knob Point, Lake Carmine.*

Bimbo put on his glasses and read the words out loud. The Queen put down her cards and listened.

"The pencil was in Otto's office?" she asked.

"On his desk," I said.

"Following the process of elementary deduction," Brains said, "it would appear that Otto was given the pencil by the real estate company. This in turn suggests that he might have done some business with this concern."

"Like renting a fishing lodge!" Bimbo said.

He lunged to his feet so violently that he knocked his chair back and it fell to the floor with a crash.

"Come on!" he yelled. "We'll go to Lake Carmine . . . to Knob Point . . . They'll tell us at the real estate office if they rented a place to Otto and where it is . . .Come on! We'll go in my car. Hurry!"

CHAPTER 18

On the Trail

As I explained before, Lake Carmine is between Crestwood and Middlebury, about twenty miles away. It didn't take us long to reach the west end of the lake, not the way Bimbo drove. All we needed was a pair of wings and we'd have been airborne.

The Queen didn't come along. I think she would've liked to but Bimbo persuaded her to stay home to look after Gulliver and Marjory. The elephant, Bimbo told us, was used to being fed promptly at five o'clock and she kicked up a fuss if her meal was late. And for an elephant to kick up a fuss might mean knocking down the whole barn.

We got directions to Knob Point at a gas station. The guy there said it was around the lake on the north side, another seven or eight miles. He pointed out what road to take.

Brains looked at his watch as we swung off the highway.

"I wish I'd left a note to my parents," he said. "We may be late getting back home . . . that is if we ever *do* get back home."

Brains had a pleasant little habit of saying things like that. I mean nobody needed to be reminded of what we might walk into. Creeps, ever since we'd taken off from the Madden house, my mind had been dreaming up enough hair-raising scenes to make a couple of TV serials.

The road we were on could have been laid out by a snake, the way it curved and looped. Trees lined either side and, in some places, their branches met overhead to make a kind of leafy tunnel. Every once in a while the road swung close to Lake Carmine. The lake was so big you could barely see across to the other side. There was no breeze to speak of and the water lay like a sheet of polished chrome. A few cottages and lodges dotted the shore but they were widely separated.

Bimbo had to cut down his speed because of the winding road. And it must have been close to five o'clock when we rounded a bend and I saw a couple of old houses and a store ahead of us. The store had a sign: HAROLD HAWKINS, *General Merchandise*. Under this was: *Knob Point Post Office*.

Directly across the road from the store was a small frame building. It was new looking, and lettered on a window was: *The MacNab Real Estate Co.*

"This is it, boys," Bimbo said. "Let's hope we hit pay dirt."

He stopped the car in front of the real estate office and got out.

"I'll go in and see what I can learn," he said.

Brains and I watched the clown walk to the front door. He took hold of the handle but the door didn't open.

"Oh, no," I groaned. "Don't tell me the place is closed."

Bimbo rapped his knuckles on the door. Then, craning his neck he peered through the front window.

"Nobody's here," he called to us.

After our hopes had rocketed so high, the news was like a knockout wallop.

Bimbo came back to the car.

"Let's ask at the store," he said. "Somebody in there's liable to know if Otto's rented a lodge in this neck of the woods."

"Good idea," Brains said.

"You boys try your luck," Bimbo said. "I think you might get better results without me."

"Very well," Brains said. "Come on, Jimmy."

As we made for the store, I kept my fingers firmly crossed. Unless we came up with some real solid info here, we'd be sunk.

The store was like the kind you find in a lot of small country towns—the walls lined with shelves of canned goods and the floor crowded with just about everything under the sun. But the main stuff for sale seemed to be fishing equipment. That figured, of course, as people mostly came to Lake Carmine to fish.

It was darkish inside and there was the smell of kerosene. Standing behind a counter was a bald-headed man, wearing a grocer's apron. And about halfway back in the store four other men were sitting listening to a radio broadcast of a ball game.

Brains went to the counter.

"Excuse me, sir," he said to the grocer. "But could you tell me if Mr. Otto Gruber has rented a cottage or a fishing lodge in these parts?"

The grocer had a cold and was sniffling.

"What's that name again, sonny?" he asked.

"Gruber," Brains said. "Otto Gruber."

The grocer shook his head. "Don't believe I ever heard tell of anybody called that," he said.

"I understand he rented a place from MacNab Real Estate," Brains said.

"Then why don't you go ask Mac?" the grocer asked.

"We did, but the office is closed," Brains said. "Perhaps you can tell us where we could find Mr. MacNab?"

The grocer broke into a laugh and so did the other men. Everybody seemed to think this was very funny.

"Yes, sonny," the grocer said. "I can tell you. First you get yourself a rowboat. Then you start out around the lake. Sooner or later you'll come on a red-nosed fella pulling in fish hand over fist. That'll be MacNab. On a day like this with the fish biting, old Mac would have to be flat on his back and dying to stay in his office."

Brains turned toward the men who were listening to the ball game.

"Do any of you gentlemen know a Mr. Otto Gruber?"

Nobody apparently did. But one man said, "Where's he from?"

"He's president and manager of the Fenton Circus. It's playing in Middlebury," Brains answered.

That didn't raise any sparks and I could see Brains' shoulders droop a little. We were getting nowhere fast and time was flying.

"He drives a foreign car," I said. "Painted bright blue."

"Oh, *him!*" the grocer said.

My heart gave a leap.

"Then you know him," I said eagerly.

"Can't rightly say I know the gent," the grocer replied. "But I've seen him pass in that furrin blue car. And he was in here once with another fella who was mad on account of I didn't carry the kind of cigars he smokes."

The Joker, I thought. It just had to be.

The grocer turned toward the group at the radio.

"Elmer," he said to one of the men, "you mind that fella in the blue car? You was sitting right there when he come in. I remember you sayin' later about all them clown heads he was wearin'—on his tie and his belt and all."

Brains flashed me a look. There couldn't be a mistake now.

The man called Elmer nodded. "Yep, I remember him."

"Wasn't he the gent Mac said he rented the Paulson lodge to?" the grocer asked.

"Yep," Elmer said. "Reckon that's the feller. Never knew his name was Goober though."

"Can you tell us where this lodge is?" Brains asked. "And how to get to it?"

"Why sure," Elmer said. "You keep on going down this here road you're on . . . maybe three or four mile. Then you come to where she forks. You take the right fork . . ."

"You go left," the grocer said.

"You go right," Elmer said.

The grocer banged his fist on the counter.

"Now lookee here, Elmer. I've been in these parts longer than you. And I ain't going to have you tell me where places are. To get to the Paulson lodge you go left at the fork."

Elmer's chair scraped as he stood up.

"Harold," he said. "I don't like to argue with a stubborn old mule like you. But you're plain crazy in the head. I know what I'm talking about."

Elmer moved toward us.

"Pay no attention to that bald-headed eagle, boys," he said. "Just do what I say. Turn right at the fork, then keep agoin' till you see a sign, SUNSET LODGE. That's it."

The grocer was coming from around the counter. He was real mad, you could tell.

I felt Brains tug my sleeve.

"Let's leave," he whispered.

We made for the door.

"Thanks for the information," Brains called as we went out.

I don't think anybody in the store heard us. For the grocer was arguing loudly with Elmer and Elmer was arguing right back at him.

We could hear them still at it when we reached the car. We scrambled aboard and Brains quickly rattled off the news to Bimbo. The clown got the car rolling right away.

"How far to the Paulson lodge?" Bimbo asked.

"Three or four miles to the fork," I said. "We don't know how far after that."

It didn't take long to reach the place where the road branched off to left and right.

"Which way?" Bimbo asked.

"That man Elmer seemed more intelligent than the grocer," Brains said. "Let's try the right one."

That was O.K. with me. I only hoped we wouldn't have to come back and go the other way.

Bimbo nosed the car into the road that veered off to the right. I sat on the edge of the seat, my heart pounding. While we'd been trying to find out if Otto had rented a lodge, I'd been able to sort of sidetrack a lot of my fears. But now they came rushing back, stronger than ever.

The road we were on cut through heavy woods. In some places the ends of tree branches slapped and scraped against the car. Once a rabbit darted across in front of us and disappeared with a leap into the underbrush. A little later, two squirrels danced out, then scooted back the way they'd come.

Now and then through the trees I could see the gleam of sunlight on the waters of the lake. The road followed the line of the shore, about two hundred yards inland.

You could have sliced the tension in the car, it was so thick. And it got worse the farther we went, with each of us straining forward to catch sight of the Sunset Lodge sign that Elmer had mentioned. Bimbo's knuckles were white, he was gripping the steering wheel so hard.

We passed one sign that read: ANGLER'S HAVEN. And another: H. T. MORRIS. In both cases private roadways led inward toward the lake. But the trees were so thick they shut off any view of a cottage or a lodge.

I figure we must have gone three miles easily and I was beginning to think we'd turn around and try that left fork when I heard Brains.

"There it is," he said.

I didn't find the sign right away because of the leaves. Then I did. It was attached to a rustic pole at the edge of the road. Letters had been formed by cut twigs and nailed to a board to spell out: SUNSET LODGE.

And right alongside the pole that held the sign was the entrance to a roadway. I couldn't see the lodge itself because of the foliage, or the lake, either.

"I'll drive on past," Bimbo said quietly, "then turn around so we'll be headed in the direction we came."

I knew he meant that we'd better be set for a fast getaway.

A little farther along, Bimbo was able to back the car around. He parked it as far off the road as possible and we got out.

"You boys better stay here," he whispered. "I'll slip up the roadway and see what I can find out."

I knew Brains wouldn't like that. And he didn't.

"We want to go with you," Brains said.

Bimbo looked uncertain.

"Now hold on," he said. "This might be dangerous. In fact, I realize now I should have got some help instead of trying to handle this thing alone."

"We'll be careful," Brains said.

Bimbo sort of bit his lip.

"Well," he said, "you can come a little way, but if things get bad, I want you both to beat it."

"Very well," Brains said.

And with that, the three of us walked back to the sign and started cautiously up the roadway that led to the lodge.

CHAPTER 19

Discovery

THE roadway was little more than a narrow lane cut through heavy underbrush. It was wide enough for one car and that's about all.

We went in single file with Bimbo in the lead, then Brains, then me. We moved slowly, keeping to the side, ready to dive for cover.

Brains and I had had plenty of scary moments in the past few days. But this to me was by far the worst. The pay-off was coming. And just about anything could happen.

Tangles of raspberry bushes crowded the edge of the roadway. There were lots of ripe berries hanging on the branches. At any other time I would've reached out and eaten some. I'm that way about raspberries. But I wasn't thinking of eating. Creeps, not now!

We'd gone maybe fifty yards when Bimbo stopped and crouched down. I saw why when we came up beside him. Ahead was a clearing where the wild shrubs and bushes had been chopped away and where grass grew. And on the far side of this clearing was Sunset Lodge.

The lodge was about the size of an average summer cottage, two stories high with a slanted roof. It had been built to look like a log cabin and was right on the edge of Lake Carmine. I could see the waters of the lake stretching out beyond.

Coming on the lodge so suddenly was startling enough. But what really rocked me was the sight of a car parked near the rear door. It was a foreign job, painted bright blue. It was Otto's, all right.

I guess all along I'd sort of wondered if we were really on the right track in spite of everything. Well, I didn't wonder any more. The car was the final proof that Otto and the Joker were here. And so, I hoped, was Skeets.

Yet, there was no sign of anybody around, in the lodge or out of it. And no sound, either.

The three of us stayed huddled close together, motionless as park statues.

I glanced nervously at Bimbo and Brains.

"What do we do now?" I whispered.

Neither of them answered for a moment. Then, Brains said,

"I suggest we get behind that shed and await developments. It should give us a clearer view of the lodge and the shore line as well."

I noticed then, for the first time, a low woodshed at one side of the clearing, fairly close to the lodge. It was almost hidden from view by a clump of evergreens.

Bimbo sized up the situation carefully. I was glad to have an older person along, I tell you. Brains was fine but sometimes he got a little reckless.

"All right," Bimbo whispered. "We should be fairly safe there. But what I said before still goes. If things get hot, I want you two fellows to bail out."

We edged around the clearing, keeping low and trying not to make a sound. There were so many trees and bushes and stuff to cover our movements that I felt we wouldn't be seen from the lodge. But somebody might hear us. It's not easy to prowl through underbrush without kicking up some noise. Fortunately, a breeze was now blowing in from the lake and rustling the leaves.

Anyway, we made it and sank down close to the rear wall of the woodshed.

Brains had sure been right about what could be seen from the new position. By peering around the corner of the shed, the side of the lodge was in plain sight and so was the shore of the lake.

The land in front of the lodge sloped down to the water. A wharf of wooden planks had been built out into the lake. And tied to an upright at the end of the wharf was a rowboat.

But that's about all I noticed, for right then an amazing thing happened. From inside the woodshed came a sharp clang. It was as if a hammer or something heavy had been dropped on metal. Then, a voice spoke from the other side of the wall where we were squatted.

"Well, that should fix it."

Creeps! I almost curled up and died. So did Brains and Bimbo from the look on their faces.

Somebody was inside the woodshed!

I'd heard Otto speak only a few times. Even so, I was positive he was the one who'd said those words. In the next second I was sure of it when another man spoke.

"Are you going to test it now, Otto?"

The foreign sound of this voice couldn't be missed. The second man was the Joker!

Brother, what a situation. After all our trouble in trying to catch up with these men, here we'd landed practically in their laps.

Maybe I kept on breathing. I must have. But that's about all I dared do. The slightest noise on our part might bring those two characters around to the back of the shed to investigate.

"Of course I'm going to test it," Otto said. "Here, give me a hand. This blasted machine's heavy."

"Do you think it's safe to leave him?"

"Why not," Otto said. "He'd have to be Houdini to get out of that rig. Anyway, we'll just be out in front and not for long, either. Lift it, will you?"

From inside the woodshed came the sound of a grunt. It was followed by the shuffling of feet.

The noise dwindled and I was almost sure they'd left the woodshed. Even so not one of us dared move. Finally

Brains crept to the corner of the woodshed and cautiously peered around it.

"All clear," Brains whispered back to Bimbo and me.

The clown and I took a look then. Otto and the Joker were trudging along the side of the lodge carrying something between them. It was an outboard motor.

We watched them go down the slope to the wharf and out on it. When they reached the spot where the rowboat was tied up, they put the motor down.

"From what Otto said, Skeets must be in the lodge," Brains whispered.

"Yes," Bimbo said. "And we've got to find him and get him out before they come back."

"Let's go then," I said.

Bimbo grabbed me by the arm.

"Hold it," he said. "We'd better make sure they aren't coming back for something."

The Joker had pulled the boat close to the wharf and had stepped into it. Otto was lowering the outboard motor to him.

"I guess it's O.K. now," Bimbo said.

We came to our feet and slipped around the other end of the woodshed to keep from being seen. I raced across the clearing to the rear of the house with Brains and Bimbo following.

"Try the back door, Jimmy," Bimbo said, his voice low.

My nerves were leaping as if they'd turned into Mexican jumping beans. Unless we got into the lodge double quick and found Skeets, we might all be caught cold.

I grabbed the knob of the back door and gave it a turn,

shoving inward at the same time. But the door didn't open.

"Bimbo," I said. "It's locked!"

"Of all the foul luck," Bimbo said. "We can't go around to the front door, they'd see us."

"Look," Brains said. He pointed up. "The window's open."

I followed the direction of his finger. About eight or ten feet from the ground was a window. It was the small narrow kind you often find in bathrooms. The lower part of it was raised.

"I could never squeeze through that space," Bimbo said.

"But I could," I said. "Boost me up."

The words were out before I quite realized what I was letting myself in for. Here I was volunteering to break into a strange house—alone!

"Get on my back then," Bimbo said. "And soon as you're inside come down and unlock the door."

He stood close to the rear wall and bent down. I climbed up on his shoulders. He straightened, giving me a sort of heave. Maybe he'd learned that special trick in the circus. Anyway it worked. I grabbed hold of the sill easy as anything and began pulling my way through the open window.

There was a bathroom in there, all right. I wriggled all the way through the window and jumped down. As I landed I heard something go *plop* on the floor behind me. I looked around and I saw that it was the rolled-up edition of the *Crestwood Daily Ledger* I'd got from Stinky. I'd forgotten all about leaving it at Bimbo's place.

I sure didn't want Otto to find a clue like that. So I picked the paper up and shoved it back into my hip pocket.

I'd have to give it to Bimbo later. One of the rules at the *Ledger* was that every paper *had* to be delivered.

Well, I beat it out of the bathroom to a hallway and down a short flight of stairs to the ground floor. I crossed a big living room that had a fireplace at one end with a bunch of stuffed fish mounted on the walls.

But I wasn't in any mood to examine trophies. All I wanted was to get that back door open and let Bimbo and Brains in. A quick look through a front window showed that Otto and the Joker were still on the wharf. The Joker was standing in the boat, struggling to put the outboard into position in the stern and Otto was kneeling on the wharf, helping him. I sure hoped they'd have a hard time getting the thing in place.

It was a cinch to find the kitchen and the back door. Then, I got a real jolt. I couldn't get the door open. It was fastened by one of those old type locks that could only be opened by a key. And there was no key.

I tried to open a kitchen window. But it was stuck fast with dried paint. Desperate now, I whirled around and hot-footed it back to the upstairs bathroom. I leaned out the window.

"Bimbo," I said in a loud whisper. "I can't get the door open. They must have the key."

I could see Bimbo wince as if he'd been slapped across the face.

"Have you seen Skeets?" Bimbo asked.

"I haven't had a chance to look," I said.

Man, this was a ring-tailed mess. Everything was going to be up to me. Then, I heard Brains speak to Bimbo.

"Give me a lift," Brains said. "I'll go in and help Jimmy."

Bimbo was in a bad spot. Here he'd been trying to protect us from danger and now he was being forced into staying on the outside looking in.

"Hurry then," he said to Brains. "I'll keep watch on Otto and the Joker."

Again Bimbo bent down and Brains climbed awkwardly on his back. I don't know how Brains ever made it up to the window. I guess his height helped. Anyway, he managed to grip the ledge. I got hold of one arm and I tugged and heaved. Finally, Brains came wriggling through the open window like a fractured eel, his glasses hanging from one ear.

He half fell to the bathroom floor. But he was up in a flash.

"Come on, Jimmy," he said. "We've got to find Skeets!"

We went along the hall. There were several doors leading off it. A couple were closed and we pulled them open. Both were bedrooms and both were empty.

"Skeets!" Brains called. "Skeets!"

He kept his voice down, but just the same I was scared Otto or the Joker might hear.

"Shhhhhh," I said. "You'd better be careful."

"The wind's blowing our way," Brains said. "They aren't apt to hear . . . *Skeets! Skeets! It's Jimmy and Brains! Skeets!*"

We were almost at the end of the hall when Brains said, "Listen!"

I froze.

Then I heard it.

"Here," a faint voice said. "In here."

The sound came from the last door. Brains fairly leaped to it. The door was closed and locked but there was a key in the hole. Brains turned it and there was the thud of the bolt going back. We both pushed the door open.

The window blind was down and it was dark inside the room. But there was enough light for me to see the boy lying on a camp cot. His arms were tied behind him with cord. And his legs were bound securely by a leather belt.

It was Skeets!

CHAPTER 20

Trapped!

BRAINS! Jimmy!" Skeets gasped.

He acted stunned, as if he couldn't believe that we were really there.

"Get that belt off his legs, Jimmy!" Brains said. "I'll free his arms. Quick!"

We bent over Skeets and I began tugging at the belt, my fingers trembling in my excitement. The belt was wrapped round and round Skeets' legs and was fastened with a big brass buckle. The front of the buckle was shaped in the form of a clown's head. I was sure the belt was the one I'd seen Otto wearing.

"Where's Otto?" Skeets asked. "And the Joker?"

"Out on the wharf," Brains said breathlessly. "Working on the outboard motor. We must get you clear of here before they come back . . . I'd better tell Bimbo!"

He whirled to the window and raised the blind. The window was in the rear of the lodge. Brains yanked it open and leaned out.

"Hissssst, Bimbo," he called softly. "We've found Skeets. He's tied up. We're freeing him."

I couldn't hear what Bimbo said. But I saw Brains nod.

He turned around and hurried back to Skeets, taking a knife from his pocket as he came.

"Bimbo's found a ladder in the woodshed," Brains said. "He'll put it up so we can escape from this window."

That was a smart idea and would save time.

Brains opened his knife and began sawing through the thick cord that bound Skeets' arms.

"How'd they capture you?" Brains asked.

"I made a bad mistake," Skeets said. "This afternoon Gulliver started barking and racing around the lab. I thought he had to go out. I figured it was safe enough. So I opened the door and went down through the garage to the outside. I intended to let Gulliver stay only a minute. But Otto was there. He grabbed me. I fought with him but he was too strong. Then the Joker drove Otto's car down the drive. Gulliver attacked them but they kicked him away, tossed me into the car and brought me here."

So that was how it had happened.

I tugged hard at the belt but I couldn't make it slide through the buckle. I was frantic. I kept listening for some signal from Bimbo outside that would mean Otto or the Joker were heading back to the lodge.

Skeets went on talking, his words coming out fast. He was all tensed up from his horrible experience and I could see marks on his face that showed he'd been crying.

"Otto was sure I knew where the paper was," he blurted. "He tried to make me tell him. He wouldn't believe I didn't know. He told me he was going to keep me here until I came clean."

Brains had the cord cut now and he yanked it away.

"Flex your arms!" Brains snapped. "Rub them to get the circulation back."

Skeets bent his arms up and down. They were stiff and I could tell they hurt him. Brains began kneading Skeet's muscles with his fingers.

A sudden banging noise came from outside the window and I jumped. But it was just Bimbo putting the ladder up.

"Hurry, Jimmy," Brains said. "Can't you get the belt unfastened?"

I tugged harder.

"I'll have it in a minute," I said. "It's stuck."

"Here, I'll cut it with the knife," Brains said.

"Don't do that!" Skeets said. "That's my father's belt. Otto was wearing it. I recognized it when he took it off to tie me up. It made everything worse knowing he'd been wearing my dad's belt all this time . . . Don't cut it!"

I pressed one thumb against the clown's head on the buckle and pulled on the leather part. I pressed so hard that all of a sudden one of the clown's ears gave way. I thought for sure I'd broken it.

But, the ear didn't break—instead, it twisted around. Then, suddenly, the front of the brass buckle snapped open and flew back. It was hinged on one side. The buckle was hollow. And tucked inside I saw something white—a piece of paper.

"Brains! Skeets!" I said. "Look!"

I pulled out the paper. It was a sheet of onion skin paper, folded many times.

"What is it?" Skeets asked.

I thought I knew and a nerve in my neck began pounding.

"Let me see it," Brains said.

He took the paper from me and went to the window.

The tug I had given the belt had loosened it. It now slipped easily through the buckle. The second Skeets was freed, he tried to stand up. But he couldn't make it and fell back on the cot.

"My legs," he said. "They're numb."

He began rubbing them hard.

"What's that paper, Brains?" Skeets asked. "Is it the one my father hid? Is it?"

Brains had the paper straightened out. I could see that there was writing on it.

"There's no doubt about it," Brains said. "It's the missing document!"

Brother! My head was spinning like crazy. We'd found it!

"There's no time to read this thoroughly now," Brains said. "But I've seen enough. Otto entered the U.S. illegally. He wasn't born here. He isn't a citizen. He could never be a citizen. He has a criminal record. When the authorities get this, he'll be deported."

No wonder Otto didn't want the paper found!

From the direction of the lake I heard the outboard motor start. It roared for a moment, then faltered and stopped. Otto and the Joker were evidently testing it. We'd have time to make a getaway.

All of a sudden I heard something else—a rattling sound as a handful of pebbles struck the window glass.

Brains stuck his head out.

"Bimbo," he said. "What . . ."

His words were choked off. He turned to us.

"Otto's coming!"

Good gravy!

I grabbed Skeets by one arm and Brains took him by the other and we helped him to the window.

"Can you make it down the ladder?" Brains asked Skeets.

"I think so," Skeets said. "I'll have to!"

"Go first then." Brains said.

Skeets slung his legs through the open window and heaved himself across the sill. Then, he started down, gripping the rungs tightly. I leaned out and saw Bimbo standing on the ground, holding the ladder.

Skeets was doing all right but his cramped muscles made him slow and it seemed to take him forever to reach the bottom.

"You go next," I told Brains. "I can catch up with you. I can run fast."

What was I saying!

Brains didn't question me. He scrambled out the window.

As soon as he was halfway to the ground, I followed.

Bimbo and Skeets were watching us from below.

"Run for the car!" Brains said. "Don't wait for us!"

They headed across the clearing. The ladder shook as Brains reached the bottom.

"Beat it after them!" I called to Brains.

Brains hesitated as if he wanted to wait for me. Then, he turned and got going.

When I was five feet from the ground I jumped. I landed hard. As I picked myself up I heard somebody yell.

"What're you doing here?"

It was Otto.

He had come around the corner of the lodge.

I began running. But so did Otto.

"Stop!" he yelled. "Stop!"

I saw that he was going to catch me unless I did something.

I guess you remember me saying what a good shot I was with a newspaper. I mean how I could throw a rolled-up edition of the *Crestwood Daily Ledger* and make it land on a doormat.

I don't know what made me think of the newspaper in my hip pocket at that moment, but I did. I pulled it out and threw it—straight at Otto's face.

If I ever wanted to hit a target, this was the time. And I scored a perfect bull's-eye. The rolled-up edition of the *Ledger* slammed into Otto, smacking him across the eyes.

He sort of staggered, let out a yell, and stumbled.

That was all I needed. I went across that clearing, going all out. I didn't look back. I swung into the roadway with-

out breaking stride. Bimbo and Skeets were far ahead and
Brains was fast catching up to them.

You can talk about Olympic trackmen setting new records. Brother, I think I would've won all the world's titles
easily if I'd been clocked that afternoon.

I heard Otto shouting.

"Joker! Joker! Come here! Get in the car."

By the time I reached the main road, Skeets and Bimbo
and Brains were climbing into Bimbo's car. Bimbo had
the engine going when I swung aboard.

"Step on it!" I yelled at Bimbo. "They're coming after us
in their car."

We shot back down the road. But as we passed the
entrance to Sunset Lodge, there was no sign of Otto's blue
job. Yet I knew it would be showing up at any second.

Bimbo drove fast for a while, then he slowed down.

"Hurry!" I said again. "Faster! They'll catch up."

Bimbo shook his head. "Don't worry," he said. "They
won't catch us. In fact, I don't think they'll even come
after us."

"What?" Skeets said.

"Why not?" Brains asked.

Bimbo grinned a little.

"While I was waiting for you, I did a little work on their
car."

He put his hand in his pocket and brought out a
brownish, circular piece of metal.

"I lifted the distributor cap and removed the rotor from
their engine," he said. "They can't get their car started, no
matter how hard they try."

CHAPTER 21

Trail's End

WE SWUNG by the Madden place and picked up the Queen, then headed fast for Crestwood. Things really began boiling over when we reached the Benton house. Brains' father was mad that we were late for dinner but he soon forgot all about eating when he met Skeets and Bimbo and the Queen and heard what had happened.

Mr. Benton called the chief of police and the chief called Washington. And Washington sent a Government agent on the double quick to Crestwood that night.

It sure was exciting having a real sleuth in the house. His name was Jim Patton and, man, he didn't kid around getting down to business. He questioned all of us, then examined the secret paper that Skeets' father had hidden.

It turned out to be just what Brains had said. It gave the low-down on Otto—facts, figures and dates. Otto had entered the country by jumping ship in New York years ago. He couldn't apply for citizenship because of his illegal entry and because of his past criminal record in England—he'd been in prison for swindling and a couple of other things. He'd known he would be deported if the Immigration Service ever found out, so he'd forged a birth certificate that he'd been born in Pennsylvania.

"You boys have done a good job," Mr. Patton said to Brains and me. "It looks as if we've got the goods on this Gruber, all right."

"But when are you going to arrest him?" I asked. "Maybe he's taken it on the lam already."

I could almost see Otto boarding a plane for South America and making a getaway.

"I don't believe he'll run off," Mr. Patton said. "In the first place he has no idea that you found this paper. Also, he knows that no kidnapping charges can be brought against him for snatching Skeets the way he did. After all, he's the boy's legal guardian. I feel quite certain that Mr. Otto Gruber has returned to the circus in Middlebury and is there right now. He's going to be a very surprised man when Uncle Sam taps him on the shoulder tonight."

Well, that's exactly what happened. Mr. Patton made a couple of phone calls, then he drove off for Middlebury. We heard later that he and two other Government agents had no trouble picking up Otto right after the night show.

Of course, the whole business got into the papers with the *Crestwood Daily Ledger* scoring a scoop over the big city dailies. I made sure of that. Brains and I had our pictures published and they gave us a front page write-up under a heading: JUNIOR SLEUTHS TRAP CROOK.

It seemed pretty clear that Otto would end up serving a jail sentence and then get deported. And it seemed clear, too, that when the investigation was over, Skeets would be the sole owner of the Fenton Circus. And you can bet when that happened, Bimbo and the Queen would be back under the Big Top again.

What with all the excitement, I didn't much care that Stony Rhodes won the grand prize in the *Ledger's* subscription contest. But at that I *almost* beat him.

The day the contest ended, Mr. Worts, the circulation manager, called me into his office.

"Jimmy," he said, "that was nice work lining up those four new subscriptions that came in yesterday. One more and you would've tied Stony for the championship. It certainly was close."

"What four new subscriptions?" I asked.

I hadn't signed up anybody for over two weeks.

Mr. Worts laughed as if I'd said something funny.

"Now don't tell me you've forgotten your new customers already," he said.

Then he showed me the names. They were:

> *Skeets Fenton*
> *Senator Fenton*
> *Gulliver Duval*
> *Marjory Duval*

It wasn't hard to guess who had arranged for the *Crestwood Daily Ledger* to be delivered to Skeets and the parrot and the dog and the elephant. It'd been Bimbo and the Queen, of course.

It's funny how a little fame changes things for a guy. When my father and mother arrived back from their visit with Ann and heard the news, they sure gave me a hand. I was allowed to stay up until after midnight telling them all the details of the case.

All of a sudden Mom got wise to how late it was.

"You'd better go to bed, Jimmy," she said. "And I'll let you sleep as late as you want to in the morning."

That suited me fine.

But do you know what happened? At eight o'clock the next morning something woke me up. It took me a little while to figure out that it was the sound of the telephone ringing downstairs.

I heard my mother answer it.

"Hello?" she said. "What's that? . . . Hello?"

My father called from the dining room.

"Is that for me, Clara?"

"No," Mom replied. "Not for you."

She sounded sort of bewildered.

"Who was it then?" my dad asked.

"Do you remember that crazy person who phoned here once before," Mom said. "Well, it must have been the same party because he said the same thing again, 'The kangaroos have escaped.'"

I fell back on my pillow. Oh, no—not another secret message from X!

I lay there for a moment. Then, I got out of bed and began dressing. I couldn't go back to sleep. Brains must have had something important on his mind. Maybe he'd uncovered a new mystery. I'd have to go find out.

After all, Operative Three of the Benton and Carson International Detective Agency must always be on the job.

Whitman CLASSICS

Black Beauty

Tales to Tremble By

Heidi

Tales from Arabian Nights

Mrs. Wiggs of the Cabbage Patch

Little Women

Huckleberry Finn

The Call of the Wild

Tom Sawyer

Robin Hood

The Wonderful Wizard of Oz

Robinson Crusoe

Wild Animals I Have Known

The War of the Worlds

Here are some of the best-loved stories of all time. Delightful... intriguing... never-to-be-forgotten tales that you will read again and again. Start your own home library of WHITMAN CLASSICS so that you'll always have exciting books at your fingertips.

Whitman

REG. U.S. PAT. OFF.

Whitman ADVENTURE and MYSTERY Books